John Creasey, (1908-1973)

John Creasey, "The King of Crime," wrote 562 crime and mystery books in 41 years, making him the world's most prolific author.*

His books have sold more than 80 million copies worldwide in 28 languages and *The Creasey Dagger* is still the UK's top award for first time crime novelists. Past winners include Patricia Cornwell and Minette Walters. Creasey's most famous characters include *The Toff*, *The Baron*, *Inspector West* and *Gideon*.

John Creasey was also the founder of the All Party Alliance in England, a political movement advocating government by the best men from all the parties working together. He fought four by-elections in 1967/68.

He advocated not only shared political control of nations but industrial democracy in which workers, management (with marketing and research staff), private investors and the State (or Federal Union) shared ownership and control of all industry and commerce. He claimed that these systems would end political strife and reduce strikes, thus increasing national prosperity to the point where the State's profit could virtually do away with income tax.

Barbara Cartland wrote more books than John Creasey—an average of eight books a year, totalling 623 in 77 years of writing. Creasey wrote 13 books per year in 41 years of writing, making him 171% more prolific.

For more about John Creasey, www.johncreasey.com

THE TOFF
AND THE LADY

John Creasey

CREASEY CRIME CLASSICS

Creasey Crime Classics
An imprint of Tethered Camel Publishing

Copyright © Siguy South 2004

The moral right of the author has been asserted

A CIP catalogue record for this book
is available from the British Library

ISBN 1-904612-02-4

Printed and bound by Selwood Printing Ltd.,
Burgess Hill, West Sussex

Jacket design by Mostra Ltd., Haymarket, London SW1

Tethered Camel Publishing
PO Box 12036, Bromsgrove, Worcs.
B60 1WT

Foreword

RICHARD CREASEY

The Toff—or the Honourable Richard Rollison—was "born" in the twopenny weekly *Thriller* in 1933 but it was not until 1938 that my father, John Creasey, first published books about him. At once the Toff took on characteristics all his own and became a kind of "*Saint* with his feet on the ground." My father consciously used the Toff to show how well the Mayfair man-about-town could get on with the rough diamonds of the East End.

What gives the Toff his ever-fresh, ever-appealing quality is that he likes people and continues to live a life of glamour and romance while constantly showing (by implication alone) that all men are brothers under the skin.

I am delighted that the Toff is available again to enchant a whole new audience. And proud that my parents named me Richard after such an amazing role-model.

Richard Creasey is Chairman of The Television Trust for the Environment *and, for the last 20 years, has been an executive producer for both BBC and ITV*

It was John Creasey who introduced him to the world of travel and adventure. Richard and his brother were driven round the world for 465 days in the back of their parents car' when they were five and six years old. In 1992 Richard led 'The Overland Challenge' driving from London to New York via the Bering Strait.

CHAPTER ONE

Mr Rollison Reads The Post

FEW THINGS GAVE Richard Rollison more pleasure than reading the post and the newspapers while having his morning tea. In far-off days it had been a ritual. Jolly, his man, who could make ritual out of scrambling an egg, would wait until he heard the first sound of movement inside the bedroom; then, as if by magic, he would appear with freshly made tea, the letters and the newspapers, neatly folded, on a large ornamental tray which Rollison said had a baroque quality more suitable to one of the more ornate hotels. It was a present from an Aunt. Nowadays the post arrived later and Rollison rose earlier than of yore; consequently it was seldom that he could indulge himself.

One September morning, however, when the skies were overcast and the heavens opened to send a deluge over London, was to be properly celebrated if the post arrived before Rollison woke up. Jolly went to the window several times to see what progress the postman was making, returning each time with the frown on his lined face a little deeper. When Jolly's face was in repose most people thought him a gloomy fellow and when he frowned he was like an apostle of gloom.

On the kitchen table the tray stood ready, glittering beneath the electric light; on the stove the electric kettle was singing and by the tray were the newspapers. Jolly looked at them as if to make sure that no intruder had disarranged them and then stepped towards the bedroom door. There was silence. His frown cleared a little. He stepped to the window and, after a moment, he looked radiant. From the house next door there came a rat-tat-tat, and then the postman appeared.

'I do hope,' murmured Jolly, who occasionally confided aloud in himself when he was alone, 'that we have a cheerful post.'

He was doubtless thinking of the fact that on the previous night— or rather, in the early hours of that morning—Rollison had been in low spirits. The weather just now would be enough to depress a saint and Jolly's only hope of a brightening prospect was vested in the post.

True, the chances were against such a fillip but it was not surprising that a man who had worked for many years for the Hon Richard Rollison believed in miracles.

The front door bell rang.

Jolly hurried to answer it, greeted the postman courteously and was given a large bundle of letters and one packet which he did not examine. In fact he forewent his usual scrutiny of the post for there came a summons from Rollison's room.

'Jolly!'

'One moment, sir,' called Jolly.

He hurried into the kitchen, put the letters with the newspapers, wetted the tea, whisked the tray from the table and, in less than sixty seconds, opened the bedroom door.

'Good morning, sir.' He stepped towards the bedside table. 'Your tea, sir. Your post. Your newspapers.'

'All,' said Rollison, his grey eyes kindling. He was lean and dark, with a thin, dark moustache and some people said that he was too good-looking and too conscious of his looks. 'That helps. What do you think of the weather, Jolly?'

'Most unseasonal, sir, but it may clear before noon,' said Jolly, serenely. 'I have often noticed, too, that when we have a wet September, October is usually a glorious month and November is almost spring-like. Would you like the fire switched on?'

'No,' said Rollison.

Jolly handed him the letters, including the package, and poured out tea. Rollison sat up in royal blue pyjamas decorated with silk lilies, his dark hair standing on end and his tanned face strikingly handsome. He switched on the lamp which was fitted to the wall above his head.

'Your tea, sir,' said Jolly.

'Thanks.' Rollison took the cup and picked up the letters one by one. 'A bill, Jolly. A letter from Aunt Matilda. A letter from Alec Gregory—he probably wants me to go down on the farm for a few weeks.' He sipped his tea, continuing to turn the letters over. 'Bill— receipt—bill—a letter from a man or woman who calls me Rawlison, posted in the East End—that might be interesting. Open it, Jolly.'

'Very good, sir.' Jolly used the paper-knife from the tray and took out the letter as Rollison continued to murmur about the others.

There were begging letters, appeals from charities, circulars, a selection of letters from relatives—in fact a surprising number. Rollison reached a bill which he thought was the last of the small letters, finished his tea and looked up.

'Well, Jolly?'

'It is from Mrs Link, sir, who hopes that you will go to supper tonight.' Jolly showed that he disapproved of the suggestion.

'Curious,' said Rollison. 'She usually only invites me on great occasions. It isn't my birthday, is it?'

'No, sir, that is in the Spring.'

'It looks as if the family is getting its happy returns in early,' said Rollison, 'I haven't known such a number of tender inquiries for a long time.'

He was holding out his cup for replenishment and relinquished his hold too soon, so that only Jolly's swift movement averted a minor disaster. 'Jolly!'

'Yes, sir,' said Jolly.

'Look at that!'

He was staring at the large envelope, and Jolly looked down, seeing the address for the first time. There was nothing really remarkable about it as far as Rollison was concerned, except that it had come through the post and been safely delivered.

'How very remarkable, sir,' said Jolly.

'That's putting it mildly,' said Rollison and peered at the postmark. '*London, WC1*, 6.15pm yesterday. Jolly, we are famous!'

'It is really most gratifying,' murmured Jolly.

The typewritten address was:

The Toff,
London, W1.

Many letters had been addressed to 'The Toff, Gresham Terrace,' but never one as briefly as this. Rollison considered it curiously as Jolly handed him the paper-knife.

The envelope was a stout one, tightly packed. The contents would not come out when the top was slit and so he slit one side and took out two pieces of thin cardboard, fastened together with gummed tape—the cardboard was almost the same size as the envelope. He cut the tape and took the pieces apart. There, face downwards, was what appeared to be a cabinet-size photograph.

Rollison looked up at Jolly.

'This looks like a family joke,' he said, 'of the kind that would seem funny to one of my less responsible relatives. Or,'—he grinned—'it might be from Lady Matilda. I sent her some rouge, lipstick and powder for her seventeenth birthday and I knew she would revenge herself sooner or later.'

'Supposing you looked at the other side, sir,' suggested Jolly.

'I'm in the mood for a guessing game. My first is Lady Matilda. What's yours?'

'If you insist, sir, I would say that it is perhaps a photograph of some film star who chooses such a method of advertisement.'

'What! With no photographer's studio emblazoned on the back? Never! As a matter of fact it looks like a newspaper print.' Rollison turned it slowly and Jolly leaned forward to get a better view.

Neither of them made any comment.

It was the portrait of a woman. Rollison, studying it carefully, judged her to be in the early thirties. She was not beautiful by any accepted standard but there was a quality about her which might loosely be termed 'lovely.' The photograph itself was perfect. The woman seemed to be there in the flesh, looking up at him with narrowed, slightly oblique eyes under long, curved lashes. Her face was rather broad and her cheekbones a shade higher than those of most English women. Her mouth, wide and full, curved a little at the corners, as if she knew this was a joke and was getting great enjoyment from it. About her neck was a rope of pearls, three strings, close-fitting like a collar. The sweep of her neck into her shoulders was loveliness itself.

After a long pause, Rollison said:

'Well, well!' He looked up at Jolly. 'No, it's not a secret passion. She is a stranger to me as well.'

'*Really*, sir?'

'Oh indubitably.' Rollison held the photograph up, to get a better light on it.

'How would you describe her?'

'I do not feel qualified to say, sir.'

'You're very non-committal this morning,' said Rollison. 'I wonder if there's a letter with it.'

There was no letter, no compliments slip, nothing except the postmark on the envelope to give any clue as to the source of the photograph. Either Jolly's interest waned or he thought it time he began to cook breakfast for he went out, leaving the tray. Rollison put the photograph on one side but glanced at it each time he picked up a letter. Most of those from his relatives were casual enough; Lady Matilda Wirrington demanded to know, in colourful terms, whether he had sent her a package intended for some wench who was not satisfied with the face which nature had given her and added a note that if he ever expected a gift from her he would be disappointed. In a post-script, which seemed a little wistful, she had added: '*When are you coming to see me, Richard?*' The bills and circulars were uninteresting, there were two begging letters and the note from Alec Gregory who wanted him to spend a week at his farm in Hampshire.

'I might even do that,' mused Rollison.

Jolly came to tell him that his bath was ready. He had not had time to open the papers and he decided to look at the headlines while he was having breakfast. He got out of bed and stretched, nearly touching the ceiling with his fingers, for he was over six-foot. As he put on his dressing-gown, however, the tassel of the cord caught in the ornamental handle of the tray. He just saved the whole contents from falling but knocked the newspapers to the floor. Absently, he picked them up. When bending down he caught another glimpse of the photograph which intrigued him greatly. Anonymous letters were not rare but an anonymous photograph had never come his way before.

Then he saw the front page of *The Record*.

A picture caught his eye and slowly he raised the newspaper for he saw that the picture was a likeness of the woman whose photograph lay on the bed. It was not a reproduction from the photograph; the angle was slightly different and the woman was not wearing her pearls but undoubtedly it was the same woman. The difference between the pictures seemed more marked the longer he studied the newspaper. Gone were the curves at the corners of the lips and the suggestion of veiled mockery in the narrowed eyes. The photograph showed something of the character of the woman; the picture in *The Record* had a blankness of expression which disturbed him.   She looked lost and forlorn.

In heavy type above the picture were the words: DO YOU KNOW THIS WOMAN? Beneath it, in italics: *To read the amazing story turn to page 3, column 1.*

Slowly, Rollison turned to page 3.

CHAPTER TWO

The Story Of The Lady

'HALLO, ROLLY,' SAID Superintendent Grice, 'I thought you had gone north after some bad men.' He shook hands with Rollison and pulled up an armchair covered in faded green cloth, then offered cigarettes. 'Couldn't you find them?'

'They were non-existent,' Rollison said, sinking into the chair. 'Thanks. You look very spruce this morning. Everyone seems to be celebrating something.'

Grice was, indeed, immaculately dressed. In his buttonhole was a white carnation, he wore a wing collar and a bow tie and in place of his usual lounge suit which always looked in need of pressing, he had on morning dress. Scotland Yard had never seen him so well turned out. Nothing, however, could alter his rather severe, even aquiline features across which the skin was stretched tightly, showing the little parallel ridges at the bridge of his nose. His skin seemed to glow; it was a golden brown, more often seen in Italians and Spaniards than in Englishmen. Brown hair and brown eyes with that delicate skin made him look almost un-English.

'One of the Inspectors is getting married at noon,' he said, 'hence the fal-de-rols.'

'Do I know him?' asked Rollison.

'I doubt it. Charters, who's just been promoted—he was in the Records Office.'

'I seem to have heard of him vaguely,' said Rollison. 'I've been out of touch for too long. Occasional descents on to the sanctum sanctorum aren't enough.' He smiled. 'I'll have to put it right. You'll soon find me at your elbow wherever you go, always ready with a word of advice. How does it appeal?'

'It sounds terrible,' said Grice.

Between these two men there was a friendship the stronger because when they had first met it had been in an atmosphere of mutual suspicion, not far removed on Grice's side from hostility. That was in the days when Rollison, so widely known as The Toff, had taken on himself the investigation of crimes with scant regard for police susceptibilities. The Toff had matured since then and the police even consulted him occasionally, although some officers at Scotland Yard could not forgive his early wilfulness. Grice knew his worth, however, and nothing seriously ruffled the calm of their association.

'As it's now eleven,' said Grice, 'I haven't a lot of time this morning. Is there something on your mind?'

'Much,' said Rollison. He took from his pocket a folded *Daily Record* and pushed it across the desk. 'Who's the lady?' he demanded.

Grice shot him a quick, searching glance.

'Can you tell me anything about her?'

'Nothing.'

'Then why are you interested?'

'Take one more look at her,' said Rollison, 'and guess.'

Grice ignored the suggestion, sat back in his chair, and pressed the tips of his fingers together.

'Now look here, Rolly, you aren't interested in her because of that photograph. It's a bad one, in any case—and you aren't the man to be intrigued by a loss of memory case unless you've a special reason.'

'Oh, I've a reason,' said Rollison, 'but before we go into that, tell me more. All I know of her I read in *The Record*. The story of the *Bal Masque*, where she turned up, is highly decorative.'

'It's true enough,' said Grice.

Rollison raised his eyebrows.

'The story isn't in any of the other papers.'

'It didn't happen until the ball was nearly over and most of the Press had gone home,' said Grice. '*The Record* still runs a gossip column and their society newshound was there, when ...'

At half-past two, when even the gaiety of a function sponsored by Mrs Barrington-Ley was beginning to lose its vitality, the lady of the photograph had arrived at Barrington House. There, Mrs Barrington-Ley had staged a *Bal Masque* on behalf of the Action Committee for Famine Relief, a generous and timely gesture. The *Bal Masque* had been one of the social events of London and even the fact that it was held in September had not affected its success. Over five hundred people had been present and the proceeds would probably reach five thousand pounds, for there had been auctions of jewellery and mock-auctions and all manner of ingenious ruses for raising money.

Everything had gone smoothly, as was to be expected of any event organised by Mrs Barrington-Ley, until half-past two when only a few dozen guests remained and most of them were beginning to collect their wraps and coats. Then into the ballroom, gay with lights and decorations, warm and filled with the haze of tobacco smoke, had come 'the lady.'

No one had seen her enter but it had been a warm night with doors and windows wide open. Taxis and a few private cars were packed outside in a long line; there had been a constant stream of guests to and from the cars. Anyone could have entered Barrington House without difficulty.

'The lady' had walked from the main doors towards the centre of the room. Half-a-dozen little groups of people had been laughing and talk-ing and the buffet, in an ante-room, was fairly full. The lady was wearing a black satin gown and over it a mink coat. There was nothing remarkable in that but her pallor had arrested the attention of the people who saw her—her pallor, said Grice and *The Record*, and her feverishly bright eyes. A dozen or more men and women had watched her and silence had fallen upon the hall when, in the middle of the floor, the lady had turned and looked about her in every direction—and then collapsed in a dead faint.

She had not come round for over an hour, by which time the police had been called, because no one present knew her.

'And is that the lot?' asked Rollison.

'It's plenty, isn't it?' said Grice.

'Yes and no. Isn't it early for you to make an appeal through the Press?'

Grice laughed. 'We didn't. *The Record* said that we would welcome any information about her, which is true enough, but we would have waited for a day or two before publicising it. I don't know that any harm's done. She says that she doesn't remember her name or where she came from, no one I've seen or we've interviewed knows her.'

'Where is she now?'

'At the Lawley Nursing Home,' replied Grice. 'Mrs Barrington-Ley decided to adopt her and shrank from the idea of her being kept at a police-station or in hospital, so she has a room at the nursing home. She speaks in a whisper and looks like a ghost. Two doctors have examined her and found nothing wrong except a bruise on the back of the head.'

'Let me have it all,' said Rollison when Grice paused.

'I'm trying to find the right word,' said Grice. 'She's tired out, suffering from physical and probably mental exhaustion. There's nothing organically wrong with her and a week's rest will probably put her right. Mentally—well, it's hard to say. If her memory's gone completely, she might be unwell for a long time.'

'Why "if"?' asked Rollison.

'How can you be sure that a stranger has lost her memory?' asked Grice. 'You can't check. We've got to take her word for it and it's early for that.'

'The natural scepticism of a policeman,' said Rollison. 'Do the doctors suggest that she might be putting on an act?'

'They're non-committal.'

'The natural self-defence of a doctor!'

'Look here,' said Grice, 'time's getting on. What made you come along?'

'This,' answered Rollison.

He took the photograph from beneath his coat and handed it to Grice, telling him everything relevant to it as Grice studied the face. Grice looked up.

'Have you got the envelope?'

'Yes,' said Rollison and took the envelope, folded, from his pocket. 'I ran over it for prints but I don't think you'll find more than Jolly's, mine and the postman's. That's curious, isn't it?'

'I suppose it is,' said Grice. 'Whoever packed it wore gloves; is that what you're driving at?'

'Yes. No one handled the photograph with bare fingers, as far as I can find out—there are only my prints on it. The mystery lady wasn't in a state of mental or physical exhaustion when that photograph was taken, was she?'

'She looks very much all there,' said Grice. 'What do you make of it?'

'Absolutely nothing,' said Rollison.

'I mean, of the photograph being addressed to The Toff?'

Rollison frowned. 'It could be that someone who knows her knows also that she is in trouble and thinks I might be able to help. It suggests that whoever knows her and had the photograph has heard a fair amount about me, and perhaps even knows me.'

'I doubt it,' said Grice. 'Otherwise it would have been addressed to you as Rollison.'

'Now, now!' said Rollison. 'That wedding is getting on your mind. What could be better calculated to make me curious than a letter addressed to "The Toff," not to Rollison? What could be better calculated to make me think that it's a matter for investigation, not just of interest? Why was I chosen and not the police? Because there is some hope that I might make private investigations—not everyone knows how friendly the Yard is towards me these days !'

Grice gave a somewhat sardonic smile.

'I thought you made nothing at all of this.'

'Inference and deduction doesn't amount to knowledge,' retorted Rollison. 'What do *you* make of it?'

'Nothing at all. I suppose you've come to me because you want to see her?'

'Any objections?'

'I couldn't keep you away if I had,' said Grice, 'but there's no reason why you shouldn't go. Of course, it may peter out. She isn't a woman whom anyone would readily forget and someone who knows her will probably turn up during the day. You'd like to know if they do, I suppose?'

'Very much,' said Rollison, getting up. 'Now you've got to go and kiss the bride—don't get tight at the reception. I may want to see you again this afternoon!'

He was in a thoughtful frame of mind when he left Scotland Yard and also a little rueful. In his wallet was an invitation from Mrs Barrington-Ley to the *Bal Masque*. He could have been there when the lady had arrived—unless, of course, he had become bored and left early.

The rain had stopped but the clouds were still lowering. He walked to Barrington House, which was in a small street off Park Lane, calling to mind all that he knew of Hilda Barrington-Ley. A charming, winsome creature who made many people think that she was featherbrained but who had helped to raise great sums of money for charities. She had hosts of friends and her husband, the banker, was extremely rich. That went without saying of the owner of Barrington House.

Barrington-Ley was twenty years older than his wife, a man of fifty-five who looked no more than forty. He was of medium height, lean and wiry. He had been frequently consulted by the Government during financial crises. As far as Rollison knew his reputation was blameless. Like his wife he was a prominent worker for various charities.

Hilda was his second wife. He had a daughter of twenty-nine, named Gwendoline, a good-looking, earnest, serious-minded girl, often dubbed a blue stocking. Rollison remembered the deep, rollicking laugh which came from her occasionally, a laugh which was quite unexpected from someone usually so sober and who gave the impression of lacking a sense of humour. There was, Rollison believed, a great affection between Gwendoline and Hilda. One other thing sprang to mind; the Barrington-Leys were often in the public eye but there was nothing about them on to which scandalous tongues could batten.

Rollison reached the house which stood in its own grounds, a Georgian residence combining all that was best of the period and containing nothing of the worst. The wrought-iron gates were open, leading to a drive with a shrubbery on either side and in front of the main entrance stood a Silver Cloud Rolls-Royce. As Rollison reached it Barrington-Ley came hurrying from the house. Rollison could not remember a time when the banker was not in a hurry. The tails of his mackintosh were flying and on his handsome face there was a look of great intensity—that, again, was usual; he always gave the impression that he was carrying a great load of responsibility. His bright blue eyes reflected a sudden, unexpected beam of sunshine which made him blink but, in spite of that, he saw Rollison and pulled up short as the chauffeur opened the car door.

'Hallo, Rollison! I didn't expect you.'

'Not unwelcome, I hope,' said Rollison.

'Great Scott, no! You're just what Hilda's been praying for—she's convinced that the police aren't trying to find out who our lost lady is. An aura of mystery surrounds her and Hilda's revelling in it. I'm warning you what to expect.'

'I can face it,' said Rollison.

Barrington-Ley put a hand on his arm and a foot on the Rolls and said earnestly:

'As a matter of fact I feel troubled about the woman — she is what you've come about, isn't she?'

'Yes. Mainly out of curiosity.'

'Good! If you can help her, I'll be really delighted.' Barrington-Ley squeezed Rollison's arm and got into the car while Rollison walked up the four stone steps and went into the hall where a footman was waiting with the door open. The footman did not recognise him and Rollison gave him his card. When he looked at it, he seemed startled.

'Mr *Richard* Rollison, sir?'

'Yes,' said Rollison.

'Only a few moments ago there was a telephone call for you, sir, and the caller gave me his number in the hope that you would be able to ring him back. Would you care to do so before I see whether Madam is at home?'

'Yes, I think I will,' said Rollison. 'What's the number?'

'Mayfair 03121, sir.'

That was his own number. As he went to the telephone in a small room to the right of the hall, Rollison thought with a smile of Jolly's resourcefulness for he had not said that he was going to visit Barrington House.

He dialled the flat and, after a moment, Jolly said:

'This is the residence of the Hon Richard Rollison.'

'Hallo, Jolly,' said Rollison. 'What's the trouble?'

'There is no trouble, sir, as far as I know, but I am very glad that I've found you. Have you discussed the matter with Mrs Barrington-Ley yet?' He sounded faintly apprehensive.

'No,' said Rollison.

'Then I wonder if it will be possible to avoid doing so for the time being, sir,' said Jolly. '*Miss* Barrington-Ley is here.'

CHAPTER THREE

Interest In The Toff

ROLLISON REPLACED THE receiver thoughtfully, stood for a moment contemplating a water-colour by de Wint and then went into the hall. The footman was waiting for him.

'Tell Mrs Barrington-Ley that I called,' said Rollison, 'and ask her whether it will be convenient for me to see her about half-past six this evening.'

'Very good, sir.'

The footman was tall and young and good-looking. He smiled at Rollison who reflected that the man's surprise when he had read the card had been a little overdone. On reflection, too, the behaviour of Barrington-Ley might be thought unusual, even for that sprightly and high-pressured man. Had they been expecting him to call?

If they knew anything about the photograph sent to him, that was reasonable.

Rollison hailed a taxi, looked out of the small window at the back several times and suddenly he leaned forward and spoke to the driver.

'Go down New Bond Street and turn into the far end of Gresham Terrace, will you?'

'Okay,' said the driver.

A small green car which Rollison thought had been following him continued along Piccadilly. Rollison smiled at his fancy, lit a cigarette and was soon put down outside the tall, narrow, grey-faced house in which he had a first-floor flat. As he paid the driver, he glanced towards the end of Gresham Terrace.

The small green car turned into the road.

'Okay, ta,' said the taxi driver.

'Are you in a hurry?' asked Rollison.

'Got to earn me living,' said the driver.

Rollison handed him a pound note.

'Wait here for me until I come out or until the little Morris moves off. If it moves before I arrive, follow it as far as the petrol in your tank will take you.'

The driver scratched his chin. He was a youthful-looking man, clean-shaven and unusually presentable.

'S'all right as far as it goes,' he said, 'but I got three pounds worth of business in my tank.' He eyed Rollison curiously and added: 'And I can't get more'n forty-five out of the cab, I might not be able to keep up wiv' the car. Fair's fair, ain't it?'

'And you're very fair,' said Rollison, giving him another two pounds. 'If you find out where the Morris is garaged, come back and report and you can also live well tomorrow!'

'Don't forget I ain't making no promises,' warned the driver, 'I'll do me best.' He nodded and turned to his driving cabin while Rollison strolled across the pavement and up the steps leading to the front door. The driver of the little car was sitting at the wheel reading a newspaper; he was nearly thirty yards away.

As Rollison put his key to the lock, the door opened and Jolly appeared.

'I'm very glad to see you, sir.' He stepped aside and then closed the door softly. Rollison stood watching him curiously. 'Can we have a word together before you see Miss Barrington-Ley?' Taking assent for granted, he walked to the door of the small spare room. Rollison followed.

'We're being very conspiratorial, aren't we?'

'I think you will agree with the need for discretion, sir,' said Jolly, firmly closing the door. 'Miss Barrington-Ley is in a state of some agitation and, although I have done my best to find out the cause for it, I have failed. However, I did manage to get some indication. I took the morning newspapers in to her, with *The Record* uppermost and folded so that she could not avoid seeing the photograph and she showed some alarm.'

'Is alarm the word?'

'If you had been with me, I am sure you would have said so,' declared Jolly. 'There was, also, some suggestion of distaste. I thought it wise that you should know before seeing her, sir.'

'Yes,' said Rollison. 'Thanks.'

'Excuse me,' said Jolly.

He went out ahead of Rollison, stepped to the front door and opened it and then said in tones of delight:

'*Good* morning sir!' He glanced at Rollison. 'Miss Barrington-Ley has been waiting for some time.'

By that time Rollison had joined Jolly and the door of the living-room had opened.

Gwendoline Barrington-Ley stood in the doorway. She was taller than either her father or her mother with an attractive figure not shown to advantage by a mannish tweed suit. Woollen stockings made her legs took sturdy. She wore a Tyrolean hat with a blue feather in the band and on Gwendoline a Tyrolean hat looked slightly raffish.

'Hallo, Gwen!' said Rollison, stepping towards her with outstretched hand.

'Have you seen my mother to-day?' demanded Gwendoline.

'Why, no,' said Rollison.

'Thank heavens for that!' She took his hand and drew him into the room. Her features were good and, with the right makeup, she would have been attractive but she scorned rouge and lipstick. There was too much powder on the side of her nose and it was nearly white — she needed a deeper shade to match her olive skin. Her grey eyes were very clear.

'Now what is all this?' demanded Rollison.

'Shut the door, please,' said Gwendoline and would not go on until he had done so. Then she burst out: 'It's that dreadful woman!'

'There are so many,' murmured Rollison.

'You know what I mean. The woman who says she has lost her memory. Lost her memory!' Her voice was biting with contempt. 'Rolly, I hate coming to you like this, I hate asking anyone to put themselves out and if this were for my sake only I wouldn't dream of it. But—well, there's mother and father.'

'Oughtn't we to start at the beginning?' asked Rollison. 'And also be comfortable?' He led her to a chair and offered her cigarettes. She drew on one deeply and, when he was sitting in an easy chair opposite her, she began to talk in a low-pitched voice, quite determined that no one outside those four walls should hear.

'I don't know when it really began. I do know that this woman is an impostor—lost memory indeed! She knows who she is as well as I know who I am. It's a trick to outwit father and she will do anything she can to make a fool of him, of that I'm *quite* sure. She'll be absolutely ruthless, too, she won't mind what trouble she causes between—'

Gwendoline broke off and bit her lip.

'This is in the strictest confidence,' murmured Rollison.

'Yes, I know, but—well, all right! Between Hilda and David.' She seemed to find it easier when she used the Christian names of her father and step-mother and Rollison needed no more telling that she looked on them both as her natural parents. 'I was there when she came in—I nearly had a fit! If you had seen David's face you would know what I mean.'

'So he knows her,' said Rollison.

'Oh yes, although he pretends that he doesn't. I often go to the London office, you see, and I was there when she came to see him, about ten days ago. Last night she looked like a ghost—on the previous occasion she looked like a Jezebel!'

'Strong sentiment,' murmured Rollison.

'Nothing can be too strong for her!'

'As I don't know the lady, I can't be judge,' said Rollison.

'You'll have to take my word for it,' said Gwendoline. 'I am quite sure that there is nothing that woman won't do if she sets her mind to it. I can only tell you that she has seen my father before and that when she left his office *he* looked like a ghost. I think she is black-mailing him but I can't be sure. I know that he has behaved most oddly since that time. Normally you can set your clock by him—oh, he's always in a hurry but he's never late for an appointment and if he says he will be home by seven or any particular time, you can rely on his getting there to the minute. That is, you used to be able to. Since he saw the woman he's been unreliable, almost irresponsible. I feel sure that he has been meeting her.'

Rollison looked at Gwendoline's flushed face and angry eyes and said deliberately:

'If you think there is an *affaire*, I can hardly interfere.'

'I don't believe that David would sink to that!' said Gwendoline. 'No, it's something much more than an *affaire* and the woman has chosen this way of wishing herself on to us. Hilda has already suggested that when she leaves the nursing home she should come to

stay with us for a week or two and David hasn't made a demur.
That's unlike him, he usually prefers to have just Hilda and me at the
house and dislikes it when we have to do much entertaining. He's a
man of very few social contacts; he spends his life at his work and the
only rest he gets is with us. Now this woman is preventing him from
getting any rest. There are times when he looks positively haunted!
I knew when Hilda suggested that she should stay that he hated the
thought and yet for some reason he couldn't refuse.'

'What prompted Hilda to be so kind?' asked Rollison.

'Her own generous heart,' said Gwendoline, and contrived to
prevent the words from sounding trite. 'She is *quite* the most generous
person alive. If there's a suggestion that anyone is in difficulties she's
on the spot as soon as she can get there. Surely you know her well
enough for that.'

'Of course,' said Rollison, although he would not have rated Hilda
quite so high. 'Well, what do you want me to do?'

'Find out the truth about this woman.'

'Anyone who claims to have lost her memory comes under the
jurisdiction of the police, you know, and they'll find out who she is
and whether she is telling the truth. They're not unused to people
who pretend.'

'Oh, the *police*,' said Gwendoline, scornfully. Then her eyes
widened with alarm. 'The police! I hadn't thought of that. You can't
tell what clumsy idiots like policemen will do or say, they haven't an
ounce of tact in their make-up. Why, they might discover that the
woman's seen David before and tell Hilda without stopping to think.'

Rollison laughed.

'You're too hard on the police.'

'I'm not,' said Gwendoline, warmly. 'I've had some dealings with
them over parking my car—they're always unimaginative and
sometimes unbelievably dense. Don't grin like that! Rolly, *will* you
help?'

'Why did you select me?' asked Rollison.

'Well, everyone knows that you're interested in mysteries and this
is a mystery. Don't forget that David is a banker of some standing.
He has a lot of influence and his support for a project, for instance,
would persuade a lot of other people to support it.

'What kind of project?'

'A loan, or a new Company, or something like that,' said Gwendoline. 'This is exactly the kind of mystery which should interest you and—well, we have *some* claim on your friendship, haven't we?'

'You certainly have.'

'Then you'll help?'

'If I can,' said Rollison, 'and without admitting that you're justified in being alarmed. Let's go back to my question—why select me? I don't think you would pay much attention to the rumours concerning me. You're not usually interested in anything that makes for notoriety. I would have put you in the category of those who strongly disapprove of my goings-on.'

Gwendoline coloured furiously.

'Well, sometimes I *have* but—well, everyone knows that you're sometimes called The Toff and that you do seem to have some influence with the police. As a matter of fact, I'm interested in the psychology of crime and I've followed some of your cases. In their way they have been quite interesting.'

'Thanks,' said Rollison, humbly. 'Have you ever written to me, Gwen?'

He felt quite sure that if she had first sent the photograph to arouse his interest, and was now following that up, he would have got some indication from her reaction. She looked blank and a little impatient and at the same time puzzled.

'I sent you the invitation to the *Bal Masque*, didn't I?' she asked. 'Why do you ask?'

'I had an unsigned letter to-day on the lines of your diatribe about the lady.'

Gwendoline sat very straight in her chair.

'I do *not* send anonymous letters!'

'People do unexpected things when they're driven to desperation,' said Rollison. 'It rather looks as if someone else takes an equally poor view of the loss of memory, doesn't it?'

'That shouldn't surprise you.'

'I suppose not. Have you ever talked to the woman?'

'No.'

'Nor met anyone who knows her well?'

'No. If I could give you any more information I would but surely you've enough to start work on.'

'I could hint broadly to your father —'

'No!' Gwendoline rose abruptly from her chair and stood over him. 'No, you mustn't do that. He would know in a moment who had put you up to it. If I thought it would do any good to question him I would speak to him myself but there must be some reason for him keeping it secret or he would have told us by now. Rolly, don't be indiscreet. I'm relying on you to—to make sure that—'

She broke off, at a loss for words. Rollison stood up and lit another cigarette for her. He promised her that if there seemed any way in which he could find out the truth, he would try to help. The suggestion of speaking to David Barrington-Ley had upset her so much that he found it necessary to talk for several minutes before she calmed down and looked at him a little shamefacedly.

'I'm afraid I've been nearly hysterical,' she said.

'Not a bit! And I'm glad you managed to stop me from talking to Hilda before I saw you. How did you find out that I might be going to see her, by the way?'

Gwendoline stared at him, wide-eyed.

'Were you at the house?'

'Yes.'

'What on earth made you go there?' demanded Gwendoline. 'Jolly told me that you were out, I'd no idea where you'd gone. Rolly! Did you know there was any reason to think that this woman was trying to influence David?'

'I hadn't a notion,' said Rollison. 'The anonymous letter included a photograph and a photograph and a story were in *The Record*. As I told David when I met him coming out of the house, idle curiosity took me along. So you see I've already an excuse for being a prodnose!'

'I can tell you one thing,' said Gwendoline. 'Nothing you say will make mother change her mind; when she's set on helping someone in distress there's just no holding her. Don't let her think that you're unfriendly towards this woman, will you? Otherwise she'll probably get difficult and be as unhelpful as she can.'

'I'll be very tactful,' Rollison promised.

He saw her to the door and she hurried down the stairs. Looking out of the window, he could just see her on the pavement immediately beneath him. She spoke to the taxi driver, who was still there. The man's words floated upwards.

'Sorry, I'm engaged.'

Gwendoline walked on and Rollison looked towards the little green car. It began to move. He stepped swiftly to the door and called for Jolly and his man appeared from the main bedroom.

'There's a taxi downstairs,' said Rollison. 'The driver's acting under my orders and is about to follow a green car that's just started after Miss Barrington-Ley. Hurry, Jolly!'

'At once, sir,' said Jolly and, taking his bowler hat and his furled umbrella from a hall-stand, he hurried downstairs. Rollison returned to the window in time to see him step into the taxi as it moved after the little green car.

CHAPTER FOUR

The Toff Meets The Lady

ROLLISON TURNED AWAY from the window and sat down. He leaned back and contemplated the ceiling, lit a cigarette and, after a few moments, hummed, *Why oh Why oh Why* with some gusto. He was not thinking about popular songs, however. He was thinking of the curious fact that the Barrington-Leys appeared to be associated with the mysterious lady and the even more significant fact that Gwendoline was greatly disturbed. Her excitement and hysteria— and in so staid a person as Gwendoline her behaviour had amounted to hysteria—had not quite rung true. It would not surprise him if she had behaved in this manner solely in order to arouse his interest— with the same purpose, in fact, as the sender of the photograph.

One fact had emerged, obvious enough and yet he had missed it before. The photograph had been sent before the lady's arrival at Barrington House. Consequently the sender could not have expected him to see another likeness in *The Record.*

The grandfather clock behind him struck one o'clock.

He sat up, stubbed out his cigarette and picked up his hat. He wished he could have followed the green Morris but there was no telling how long that trail would take.

He had lunch at a small restaurant which served the flat in Gresham Terrace and then took a taxi to the Lawley Nursing Home, which was in Grosvenor Place. He was most anxious to meet the lost lady.

A stately, well-preserved woman in a navy blue dress received him. With his card in front of her, she was very gracious; how could she help Mr Rollison?

Rollison said, mildly, that he would very much like to see the patient who had lost her memory.

'Why, do you know her?' asked the stately woman, who was the matron.

'I think I might,' murmured Rollison.

'I do hope you do,' said the stately woman. 'We all feel so desperately sorry for her, Mr Rollison; we have had some experience of amnesia cases, you know, and I assure you that there is nothing more distressing. She is not well, of course, but we have little doubt that she will soon be *physically* herself. As for her memory—'

'Time will tell,' said Rollison.

'Exactly! And if she sees someone whom she knows, it might bring everything back to her. You won't mind if I come with you, I hope? I can watch the patient closely when she sees you. I'll first make sure that she is awake,' the matron added, 'it would be a pity to disturb her if she has fallen asleep.'

'If she has, I'll come again later,' said Rollison.

He waited in the office while the matron was out and he looked about the room with casual interest. There were photographs of royalty and other distinguished patients and on every hand there were evidence of a discreet effort to impress visitors.

After five minutes he began to fidget. At the end of ten minutes he stood up and almost immediately the door opened. A young nurse who looked a little scared entered, coughed in some confusion and said:

'Matron says, sir, if you don't mind, sir, perhaps it would be better if you were to come back tomorrow morning.'

'Tomorrow,' ejaculated Rollison.

'Yes, sir. This way out, sir.'

'What room is the patient in?' asked Rollison.

'Number 4, sir, this way out, sir.' She led the way to the front door and only when she reached it did she realise that Rollison was going in the opposite direction. She exclaimed in concern. Rollison ignored her; he had seen that the door of a room on the ground floor was marked 4. As he stood outside it for a moment the nurse came back, speaking in a low-pitched but appealing voice: the patient could not be allowed visitors that day. Rollison held up his hand and succeeded in silencing her as he listened to the murmur of voices from the room beyond. First there were two voices, then only the matron's, raised a little so that he could hear every word. She was holding a disjointed conversation.

'Yes. …Yes, doctor, she was perfectly all right at half-past two and had a good lunch … Her pulse is very low and she is running a hundred-and-one … One, yes. … Yes, *complete* coma.' There was a longer pause, before she went on: 'I have done all that, doctor … In half-an-hour, that's splendid.'

After she finished there was the *ting* of the telephone being replaced.

Rollison put his fingers on the handle of the door.

'Oh, *please*!' appealed the nurse.

'I shall tell matron that you did all you could to stop me,' promised Rollison, and opened the door.

The matron was standing by the side of a single bed, in a room where everything was white or green. A nurse in starched cap and white dress was standing with a hand on the forehead of the woman who lay on the enamel-painted bed, a woman whose pallor was so marked that Rollison drew in his breath in surprise. The sound made the matron swing round.

'Hallo,' said Rollison. 'Serious trouble?'

'You shouldn't be in here!' whispered the matron. 'Go out at once.'

'Not just yet,' said Rollison. He gave her a most charming smile and approached the bed. There he stood looking down on the woman of the photograph. Because of her pallor she was remarkable. Apart from it, she looked as she had done in the newspaper photograph and he got the impression that all vitality, all personality and charm had been drawn out of her. She seemed hardly to be breathing. Her high cheek-bones looked more prominent than in his photograph and her lips were parted slightly. Now that he saw her with her eyes closed, the fact that they sloped upwards a little towards the temples confirmed his first impression-that she was not English.

'Mr *Rollison*!' said the matron, sharply.

'I'll come into your office,' said Rollison but instead he stepped across the room and examined the window carefully. The day had turned warm and the window was wide open. It was of the modern type with a patent, self-locking fitting and, when ajar, could easily be opened from the outside. He stood there for some moments and then turned to the cabinet by the side of the bed.

'Has anything been touched since you found her?'

'No, of course not,' said the matron while the nurse looked at him with startled curiosity. 'Mr Rollison, I must insist—'

Rollison ignored her and picked up a medicine glass. There was a little green liquid at the bottom.

'What time did she take this?'

'After lunch. I positively must insist—what are you doing?' The matron's voice rose a shade as Rollison took a folded handkerchief from his pocket, wrapped it about the glass and stuffed it back in his pocket. 'You have no right to do that!'

'I want to make sure that nothing happens to it before the police arrive,' he said.

'The—police!'

'Obviously we must tell them of this at once,' said Rollison and his expression was bleak. 'It isn't nice and it might be murder. But then, you know that, don't you? What are the symptoms?' When she did not answer, he went on: 'Acute narcotic poisoning, aren't they?' He judged her agreement from her expression and nodded. 'I was afraid so. Have you any men on the staff?'

'We—Mr Rollison!'

'Have you?' insisted Rollison, and added very gently: 'The nursing home has an excellent reputation, matron, and I should not like anything to happen which would cause it harm.'

The matron became almost as pale as the patient.

'We have—two porters.'

'Have one of them stand outside the window and make sure that no one attempts to force an entrance,' said Rollison. 'Have the other outside the door with the same instructions. I'm afraid it's a case of locking the stable door after the horse has gone but it might come back, you know. Will you do what I ask?'

'I suppose you know what you're doing,' she said. 'I will send for them at once but *please* come out.'

'Will the nurse be here all the time?'

'Yes.'

'Good. It isn't likely that the patient will come round but if she shows any sign of returning consciousness, send for the matron at once, nurse. And remember, that if she should utter even a single word, it might be helpful.'

The nurse promised hoarsely that she would do what he said. She looked as frightened as the matron, presumably worried so much because there had been a serious lapse of discipline. He followed the matron out of the room. The little nurse was waiting outside, obviously apprehensive. The matron gave her instructions to send the porters to the office and, maintaining her stately poise, she walked to the office and sat down at her desk. She was inwardly in a state of great agitation.

'What else has gone wrong?' demanded Rollison.

A tinge of colour stained the woman's cheeks and he admired her as she pulled herself together and answered.

'She should not have been left. The police asked us to arrange for a nurse to be with her all the time and the doctors were equally emphatic. Nurse Armitage, who was on duty, was taken ill and we could not find another at short notice who was free. It was only a matter of half an hour that the patient was left. She was well enough at lunch because I was there with her myself.'

'I see,' said Rollison.

'What is your interest in her?' asked the matron, now rallying well. The shock of the discovery had temporarily unbalanced her for if the patient died some blame would undoubtedly be attached to the nursing home. Now, however, she resumed her cloak of authority.

'I think she is a friend of a friend,' said Rollison, evasively. There was a tap at the door and the porters came in, two ordinary men in white smocks. The matron gave them precise instructions, dismissed them and turned to Rollison.

'Why were you so—officious?'

'Someone had to make sure that everything necessary was done,' said Rollison. He touched the little bulge which the medicine glass made in his pocket. 'That would probably have been washed and someone might have closed the window. Should that have been left open?'

'Not at the bottom—there is a special ventilation shutter at the top. The nurse on duty was careless and I didn't notice it. I should have done, of course; the responsibility is mine.

'I wonder if it is all yours,' murmured Rollison and, having won her hopeful interest, he went on: 'This nurse who was taken ill— where is she?'

'She has gone home.'

'Has she been with you long?'

'Only a few weeks.'

'Have you found her quite satisfactory?'

'Perfectly,' said the matron, who obviously caught the drift of his questions. 'I do not think that she co-operated with the people who administered the poison—if there *was* a poison. We are speculating and I really cannot allow it, Mr Rollison. It may be a natural illness, a result of the prostration or of some trouble which had not been discovered. I really can't assume that the patient was poisoned. She was to have had a dose of *Neuro-Phosphates* before tea—before all meals—so that was quite in order. The drop of liquid at the bottom of the glass was green, wasn't it?'

'Yes,' said Rollison.

'Then it is almost certainly *Neuro-Phosphates.*'

'Where is the bottle from which it was taken?' asked Rollison and, when she hesitated, he added: 'I saw the police before I came here, they won't object to these questions.

'The bottle is in our dispensary,' replied the matron. 'It is frequently prescribed and we have it in bulk quantities.'

'Can I see it?' asked Rollison and then changed his mind, anticipating a refusal and avoiding it. 'No, that can wait for the police, provided it is put aside and not touched again until they've examined it.'

'I will see to that,' said the matron. 'I suppose I'd better do it myself. Is there anything else you would like?'

'Several things,' said Rollison, 'including a word with the police. May I use the telephone?'

She said 'Yes,' not very graciously, and went out. Rollison dialled Whitehall 1212, but did not wait to speak to Grice. He left a message which should bring Grice here hot-foot, rang off and moved to an oak filing cabinet by the side of the desk. He was not in view of anyone who might pass the window but he looked at the door from time to time as he pulled open the filing cabinet and ran through the manilla folders inside. Under 'N' he found '*Nurses.*' On the matron's desk was a time-table of duties which confirmed that Nurse Armitage had been on duty in Room 4 that afternoon. He picked out the card about Nurse Armitage, reading:

Armitage, Phyllis Jane, 6a Leeming House, White Court, Kensington.

Age: 26.
Certificates: SRN.; SCM.
Previous experience: Castle Nursing Home, Leamington Spa.
Seaview Maternity Home, Bournemouth.
References: Attached. Excellent.
Reports: After 1 month, most satisfactory.

He read the address again, murmuring to himself: '*Phyllis Jane Armitage, 6a Leeming House, White Court, Kensington, aged 26.*' Then he replaced the folder, without looking at the various letters attached, and closed the filing cabinet. His hand was on the telephone when the matron came in, carrying a large bottle of a clear green liquid and a white record card.

'I have it,' she said, unnecessarily. 'The contents are quite uncontaminated, as far as I can find on a quick analysis, Mr Rollison.'

'I didn't think they'd try to polish off the entire nursing home,' said Rollison, mildly. 'The police will be here soon. Would you prefer to tell them what happened or shall I wait?'

'I would *much* prefer to be on my own.'

'Then I won't embarrass you,' said Rollison. 'Will you tell Superintendent Grice that I have the medicine glass?'

She was obviously about to ask him to leave it behind but he smiled at her from the door and disappeared before she could protest. She sat back and looked at the door, frowning, still greatly upset and she was sitting like that when the police arrived.

In his taxi Rollison took out the glass, sniffed the contents but recognised no particular smell. He put a two-shilling piece into the glass, so that it lodged itself half-way down, like a stopper, then carefully wrapped it up again in the handkerchief and put it back in his pocket, lodged against his wallet so that it could not move on its side. Grice would not like him taking the glass away and would express himself colourfully if the dregs of the dose were lost.

The taxi turned off Bayswater Road into Queen's Road and, a little way along, pulled up sharply as the driver saw the nameplate on the wall of a narrow turning—*White Court*. There was just room for the taxi to get into the Court and beyond there was plenty of room for a cab or a small car to turn when on full lock. White Court consisted of a dozen tall, drab-looking houses, packed tightly together. Only one of them had been painted recently. Outside it hung a notice board: *Leeming House—Furnished Flatlets.* Rollison saw that as they passed a laundry van drawn up just outside Leeming House; and then he forgot it for parked behind the laundry van was a small green-painted Morris car.

CHAPTER FIVE

Phyllis Jane Armitage

'CAN'T GET BY the house, mister,' said the taxi driver, 'I'll have to drop you further back.'

'As far back as you can, please,' said Rollison. 'And wait, will you?'

The cab pulled up. As Rollison climbed out a sombre figure, dressed in black, appeared in the doorway of one of the houses. He did not venture far into the *cul-de-sac* but attracted Rollison's attention by raising his furled umbrella. Rollison joined him and smiled a greeting.

'Where lone trails meet, eh, Jolly?'

'They appear to, sir.'

'How long have you been here?'

'A little more than an hour.'

'Where's the taxi?'

'Waiting for me in the main road, sir. I thought it best to make sure that I had some means of transport available.'

'Quite right,' said Rollison. 'What else?'

'There is nothing of great moment,' said Jolly. 'The driver of the car is a good-looking young man of quite pleasant aspect. After leaving Gresham Terrace, Miss Barrington-Ley secured a taxi. I expected that the young man would follow her but he did not. He went to a popular restaurant and had lunch and I thought it wise to do the same and thus to keep him under my eye. He gave me no reason for thinking that he knew that he was being followed, sir, and I am sure that I did not attract his attention. From the restaurant he went to an office in the Strand—I have the address and I was able to find out which office in the building he visited. It was a firm of accountants, sir, next door to a firm of solicitors of the same name.'

'I see,' said Rollison. 'And then?'

'He was there for some time but I thought it might be wise to wait and follow him to his next destination,' said Jolly. 'He left the office a little after four-forty-five and came straight here. It is now nearly six o'clock. I am afraid'—Jolly looked apologetic—'that I have not yet discovered which particular flatlet that young man has visited.'

'He might live there,' Rollison said.

'I think it unlikely, sir. He spent some time looking at the board on to which the cards of the residents are pinned. After he had done that, he first left his car outside, sir, and I followed on foot—he went out and brought the car into the Court. On that occasion he gave me the impression of being very pleased with himself.'

'So he's found his quarry,' mused Rollison.

'Presumably. May I inquire what brought you here?'

'Someone has no love for the mysterious lady,' said Rollison, 'and the someone may be Nurse Phyllis Jane Armitage, of Flatlet 6a. Stay here, and if the man comes out alone, follow him.'

'Supposing the lady comes out alone, sir?'

'I'll follow her,' decided Rollison.

He walked close to the walls of the houses so that he could not be seen easily, nodded to his cabby, who was reading a paper-covered book, and entered the gloomy doorway of the house. It was gloomy because the landing windows were boarded up but it had recently been repainted and there was a smell of paint in the passage. On the first floor landing two men in overalls were busy on the woodwork. They paused and wished him good-day. He nodded amiably but wished them anywhere but at Leeming House. However, when he reached the next floor and glanced down, he saw that they were beginning to pack up for the end of the day's work.

On that floor was Flatlet 6a.

It was one of two flatlets on the right-hand side of the landing; those on the left-hand side were numbers 5 and 5a. Except for the murmur of voices from the workmen there was no sound, although he pressed his ear close to the door of the nurse's flat in the hope of hearing a snatch of conversation. Instead, he could get no confirmation that anyone was inside.

He hesitated before he examined the lock of the door. It was old-fashioned and anyone with a pen-knife and some dexterity could open it. He had a pen-knife...

The front door opened on to the small, gloomy hall, a box of a place from which two doors led. Both doors were closed. Now he could hear the murmur of voices and one of his fears—that the nurse might have been hurt—faded. He stepped close to the door from which the voices were coming and heard a girl say sharply:

'Must I tell you again? No!'

'Now look here, Phyl,' began a young man.

'I will not do anything more!' declared Phyllis Armitage and, judging from the tone of her voice, she was on the point of losing her temper. 'I wish I'd had nothing to do with it at all! I was a fool. Why, I might lose my job and my references, I might even have my certificates cancelled!'

'Oh, nonsense! You couldn't help being ill.'

'I'm *not* ill.'

'No one else knows that,' said the man. 'Honestly, Phyl, you'll be doing a lot of people a good turn if you'll go back and take on night duty.'

'I said no and I meant no. They'll realise at once that I was malingering if I get back by eight o'clock. Even if I were to go, I can't be sure that they would post me to her room. And if I did go back and they did post me to her room and she talked all night, I wouldn't pass on a word to you.' She sounded almost in tears.

The man spoke again.

His voice had altered and Rollison frowned as he heard the words, carefully uttered and with just the degree of menace which might be expected to take effect.

'You know, Phyl, now you've started, you can't very well back out.'

'What—what do you mean?'

'Supposing someone was to drop a hint that—'

'You—*beast!*' cried Phyllis Armitage. There followed a sharp sound; very much like a slap and a thud, as if the slap had taken the man by surprise and he had staggered back against the wall. There followed another silence, broken only by the laboured breathing of the girl.

Then: 'You'd better be careful,' said the young man who, according to Jolly, had a pleasant countenance. 'You'll fly into a temper once too often. I won't try to make you see sense any more to-night but you'll go on duty to-morrow *and* you'll do what I ask you.'

The girl did not answer.

'Or you'll have cause to regret it,' said the young man, and there was the sound of footsteps.

By then Rollison was at the front door. He went out but did not close it. He stepped up the stairs and reached the next landing before the young man appeared. He caught a glimpse of fair, curly hair and a round, ingenuous face, on which was a look of some surprise. Rollison stepped out of sight. The young man stood on the landing for some time and then he seemed to make a decision for the door closed with a snap and he walked quickly down the stairs. By the time Rollison was on the landing again, an engine was starting up in the Court. The boarded windows prevented Rollison from looking out but he felt sure that Jolly would not lose the man and he knocked at the door of Flatlet 6a.

There was no immediate answer.

He knocked again. The knocker was a small one of brass and there was no bell. If the girl were in the inner room, she might not hear, unless the inside door were open. He gave her a minute by his watch, then rapped loudly.

He heard her footsteps in the hall.

When she opened the door, she backed away, startled at the sight of a stranger, although the stranger was smiling. Her face was pale and she looked as if she had been crying. He thought she had hastily wiped her eyes and put on powder which was more expertly applied than Gwendoline's had been.

Phyllis Jane Armitage was better looking than Gwendoline Barrington-Ley. She was fair and her hair was in loose, probably natural curls, making her head look round. Only a nose which was nearly snub prevented her from being really lovely but it was somehow the right nose in the right place. The look of surprise on her face was not altogether because of Rollison—she had an air of perpetual surprise.

'Good evening,' said Rollison.

'Good evening.'

'May I see Miss Phyllis Armitage?'

'I am Miss Armitage.'

'Then I hope you can spare me a few minutes,' said Rollison and walked past her into the hall. She looked still more surprised but did not protest. She closed the door, glanced at him curiously and then led the way to the room where she had talked with the young man. Almost the first thing Rollison saw was a man's cigarette case, large enough to hold twenty cigarettes, on a small table by the side of an easy chair.

The flatlet was comfortably and pleasantly furnished. There was good taste in the flowered cretonnes at the windows and loose covers of the same material on the three easy chairs and a pouffe in front of the electric fire. A small gate-leg table stood in the middle of the room, a console radio was the most expensive piece of furniture there—it was in a corner, with a vase of antirrhinums and phlox on it.

Rollison handed the girl his card.

He did not think she had ever heard of him and he felt quite sure that she had not sent him the photograph.

'I don't quite understand why you have called,' she said.

'I hope I will be able to save you trouble,' said Rollison, and accepted a chair which she touched. As she sat down opposite him she looked apprehensive and he went on: 'I've come from the nursing home.'

She was immediately on the defensive. 'I have never seen you there.'

'I hadn't been there until this afternoon,' said Rollison. 'Miss Armitage, there was an unfortunate incident after you left. Your patient was taken seriously ill.'

As she sat back aghast, she seemed all eyes. There was green and blue and grey in those eyes which were glistening as if it would not take much to make her cry.

'The illness probably won't prove fatal, but it might. In any case, the police will make close inquiries into what happened while you were in the room with her and why you left at such short notice.'

'I—I was taken ill.' The words lacked conviction. She had been allowed no time in which to collect herself; had he spoken to her an hour later, she might have managed to sound convincing.

'Were you?'

'Of course! I had permission to leave!'

'You don't look ill.'

'You are impertinent!' she snapped, but he thought her resistance was likely to collapse at any moment.

'I don't think impertinent's the word,' Rollison said, gently. 'The police will make sure that they get the truth, you know, and they will think it odd that you show no signs of illness now.'

'Are—are you a policeman?'

'No, I'm responsible only to myself,' said Rollison, 'and what I learn I can keep to myself. Why did you pretend to be taken ill?'

He was afraid that she was going to be stubborn even now. If he was to help her, and he was quite sure that she badly needed help, he needed her confidence and trust. So he sat back, smiling at her invitingly while she fought her battle. He could see the changing thoughts in the expression of her eyes. Abruptly, she said:

'I did it to help a friend.'

'How could it help anyone?' demanded Rollison.

'A friend of mine knew—knew about the patient who has lost her memory.' She was talking quickly, rather like a child anxious to be finished with a recitation which it had been learning with great difficulty. 'He said that he thought he knew her but wasn't sure. He wanted to look at her. He could have done that through the window, of course, but—well, he said that a quick glance wouldn't be any good. He suggested that I left the room without telling anyone. Then if another nurse entered the room and saw him there it wouldn't be serious for me, as I was supposed to be ill. I let him persuade me. Once I'd left the room and said that I was unwell, I had to keep up the pretence. Matron sent me home. That is all I can tell you.'

'Except the name of the friend,' said Rollison.

She set her lips tightly and did not answer.

'Isn't that mistaken loyalty?' asked Rollison.

She did not answer.

'You'll have to tell this story to the police,' said Rollison, 'and they'll insist on knowing who it was. If you refuse to tell them they will think the story is a false one; assume that you administered the poison to—'

'Poison!' gasped Phyllis. 'Are you sure?'

'Yes,' said Rollison. 'I am quite sure.'

'Poison!' she exclaimed again, and she rose from her chair and looked at him, her eyes rounded with horror and her breathing quickening. She held her hands up in front of her, as if to fend off an evil thing. 'I—didn't dream—' she continued and then she turned away and stepped to the window, where she stood looking out on the dreary house opposite. 'I can't believe that Marcus would do that!'

'Someone did, this afternoon,' said Rollison.

She said: 'I can't believe that Marcus would do anything like that. He's cruel sometimes and—but that has nothing to do with it.' She swung round, suddenly angry. 'I believe you're lying to me! I believe you're trying to make me say too much, that you want to make me incriminate myself.'

'Now don't talk nonsense,' said Rollison. He stood up and went to the window by her side. 'I would like to help you. I have an interest in the lady in question, too, and I shall have to go on making inquiries whether you are free or not. If you tell me and then the police the whole truth, you won't be detained.'

'How—how do you know?'

'They would need more evidence than that would give them,' said Rollison. He put his hands on her shoulders and made her look at him. Her eyes were bright and her face had a freshness and vitality which her fears and terrors then could not wholly hide. She was trembling but she faced him frankly as he went on: 'If there is anything in your story that it wouldn't be wise to tell the police just now, I'll tell you so. Seriously—I want to help.'

'I don't see why you should,' she said.

'But you think I do, don't you?'

After a pause, she slipped away from him and stepped to the table, where her handbag lay open. She took out a cigarette case and lit a cigarette, without once looking at him. She coughed when the smoke caught at her throat.

'I suppose so,' she said. 'Marcus—Marcus Shayle is a friend of mine.'

'Did he give you any other explanation of his anxiety to look at the lady?'

'No, I've told you all I know,' she said, 'except—oh, I know I shouldn't have let him go there, I should have refused to have anything to do with it! But there seemed no harm and Marcus—well, he's engaged to my sister.'

'I see,' said Rollison.

'Need I tell the police that? I don't want Janice to be brought into this if I can help it, she's—she's younger than I, it might upset her and—' She paused, miserably, and then asked: 'Can you see what I mean?'

'Yes,' said Rollison. 'But they'll soon find out that he is engaged to sister Janice, you know. The police had better be told everything but your best attitude is one of repentance. It was an odd request; you knew that you shouldn't have acceded but Marcus was a friend and you saw no real harm. Then when you had left the room you realised that if the matron discovered that you weren't ill it might get you into trouble, so you decided to carry the thing through properly. That isn't so far from the truth, is it?'

'No,' she said. 'But it will make it look as if Marcus gave her the poison.'

'If he didn't give it to her there is nothing to worry about and if he did the sooner we know it the better,' said Rollison.

'Is Marcus Shayle a curly-haired man with a round, rather boyish face?'

'Yes,' she said. 'I suppose you saw him as you came up.'

'I saw him in the street. What did he want here?'

She told him, filling in the gaps of the conversation, although Rollison had heard all that really mattered while listening at the door. At first Marcus had said he much appreciated her help and promised it would not get her into difficulties at the nursing home. After she had made tea, he had broached the subject of her returning to take up night duty so as to make a note of everything the woman said.

When she had finished, Rollison asked:

'How long has your sister known Marcus?'

'Not very long,' she said. 'Two or three months.'

'Before you went to the nursing home?'

'Yes but after I had applied for a post there,' said Phyllis. 'What has that got to do with it?'

'Nothing, probably,' said Rollison. 'How long has he known where you worked?'

'Well—since I started, of course. In fact since I interviewed matron and she offered me the post. That can't have anything to do with this, can it?'

'I don't see how,' admitted Rollison.

As he spoke a car drew up outside with a squeal of brakes which startled the girl. Rollison leaned forward, and saw the top of a Wolseley. A moment later Grice and two of his men climbed out of the car. Rollison turned hastily.

'The police are here. Tell them the truth, as we've discussed it. If they ask whether I've been here you can tell them but there's no need to volunteer the information. And don't worry too much!' He was walking across the room as he spoke, and he picked up the man's cigarette case and slipped it into his pocket.

'That belongs to Marcus,' Phyllis said.

'I hoped it did,' said Rollison: 'He'll get it back.' He stepped to the front door. As he opened it he heard footsteps on the stairs. Then a door opposite Flatlet 6a opened and a man in painter's overalls appeared. He seemed taken aback at the sight of Rollison and darted behind the door again. As he did so he slid his right hand into the capacious pocket of his overalls, but he was a shade too late to hide the gun in his hand.

CHAPTER SIX

No Murder

THE DOOR SLAMMED. The footsteps of the police reached the first landing. Rollison raised his voice and there was an urgent note in it.

'Grice! Stop the painter in overalls at the back!'

He put his left shoulder to the door behind which the man had disappeared. He was handicapped because of the glass in his pocket—if he shook it too much the two-shilling piece might move and the liquid would splash up to the handkerchief and be soaked up. The door sagged under his pressure. On the landing below Grice was calling orders to his men. As the door sagged still further, Grice came rushing up the stairs and the door of Phyllis Armitage's flat opened.

'Finish this off, will you,' said Rollison to Grice and stood aside. Grice put his whole weight behind the effort and the door burst open.

As he staggered inside, Grice muttered: 'I hope you've good grounds for this.'

'A man with a gun and intent to murder,' said Rollison, and stepped past him towards a room which looked exactly the same as 6a. The window was wide open and a gentle breeze coming through. He looked out in time to see the man in overalls jump from the ladder to the pavement and run towards Queen's Road. At the same time Grice's two men reached the street and raced in pursuit.

Grice reached the window in time to see his men disappearing. He drew back as Phyllis came into the room.

Rollison beamed. 'Miss Armitage—Superintendent Grice, of New Scotland Yard.'

'How do you do,' said Phyllis, calmly enough.

'Er, good evening.'

'May I inquire what is happening?' asked Phyllis and her turned-up nose helped to give her just the right expression of ingenuous bewilderment. 'There's no one in this flat—the tenant has gone away for a week.'

'There was someone inside,' stated Grice.

'About whom we shall tell you in due course,' said Rollison who felt on top of the world. 'I think the Superintendent wants a few words with you, Miss Armitage.'

She still looked puzzled. 'Of course,' she said and went back to her own rooms, leaving both front doors ajar.

Grice had changed into a brown lounge suit and looked much more comfortable. There was a note of acerbity in his voice.

'I thought I'd find you here when I heard you'd been to the nursing home,' he said.

'Prophecies all coming true,' said Rollison, 'and yet you always say you don't believe in hunches.' He unbuttoned his pocket as he spoke.

Grice said: 'What have you said to the girl?'

'You didn't give me time to say much,' said Rollison. 'Another ten minutes and I would have got the whole story out of her. Here's a present for you. I don't mean the florin,' he added as he held the medicine glass out. There was still a little liquid at the bottom when he tilted it. 'Go on, it won't bite—didn't the matron tell you I'd taken it away?'

'Yes,' said Grice. He took the glass and put it on the mantelpiece. 'Why did you take it?'

'Curious disquiet at nursing home,' said Rollison. 'It may have been genuine alarm at the collapse of "the lady," or it might have been because they have failed to carry out police and doctors' instructions but it might also be because they harbour deep and guilty secrets. I didn't intend to take any chances with that glass—although it probably contains nothing but *Neuro-Phosphates*.' The bantering note faded from his voice as he added: 'How is the lady?'

'It will be touch and go,' Grice answered. 'They think they'll pull her round.'

'No murder yet,' said Rollison. 'Here nor there.'

'You're in an infuriating mood,' said Grice. 'Here or there what?'

'No murder,' said Rollison. 'Man with gun dressed as a painter was almost certainly after our demure little lady here. She has a very pretty face, not at all a bad figure and something of the air of an *ingenue* which I think is natural and unassumed.'

'You always did fall for a pretty face,' said Grice.

'That's uncalled for, unfair, unjust and quite true,' declared

Rollison. 'See what you can find out from her. I don't think she will
keep much back. I do not think that she left the mystery lady's room
on a pretext but I shouldn't read too much in that. By the way, what
doctors attend "the lady"?'

'Renfrew, of Wimpole Street, and Cray.'

'Renfrew as Mrs Barrington-Ley's society nominee, I
suppose,' said Rollison. 'Cray put up by the Yard.'

'Why do you ask?'

'Curiosity,' said Rollison.

'You're unbearable,' said Grice. 'Are you coming in with me to
talk to this girl?'

'No, I must be off. I promised to call on Hilda to-night.'

'Mrs Barrington-Ley?'

'Yes. Good hunting!' Rollison smiled and led the way out of the
room.

As he reached the landing one of Grice's men appeared on the
landing below. The man came up when Rollison beckoned him and
reported that the pseudo-painter had managed to get away but that
Sergeant Miller was trying to find out where he had gone.

Grice was about to tap at Phyllis Armitage's door and Rollison was
half-way down the stairs when he stopped, turned and called:

'Oh, William?'

'Yes?' said Grice, also turning.

'How was the wedding?'

Grice glared. Rollison, smiling as if he thought he had cracked a
brilliant joke, continued down the stairs and into the street. There
was a chance that Jolly had succeeded in tracing Marcus Shayle's
home and therefore a chance of seeing the man before the police
reached him. Hilda could wait until he had heard from Jolly. He
called his taxi and, in a voice loud enough for Grice to hear, gave him
the address of Barrington House, changing it only when they were in
Bayswater Road.

Beneath his good mood there was an underlying note of uneasiness.
Even if the case resolved itself fairly well and Marcus Shayle had
poisoned the lady of lost memory, much would remain unsolved and
there would be danger to both the unknown woman and to Phyllis
Armitage. It was disquieting to think that a man had been waiting in the

neighbouring flatlet, doubtless with the intention of murdering Phyllis. The man had probably postponed action because he knew that Phyllis had a visitor but then been forced into the open. From these conclusions it was reasonable to suppose that Marcus Shayle and others were most anxious that Phyllis should not disclose the story of her actions that day.

Jolly had not yet returned to Gresham Terrace. It was then nearly half-past seven and Rollison telephoned Barrington House, asking for Hilda. A man with a stilted voice regretted that Madam was out. So, it proved, were David Barrington-Ley and Gwendoline. He had been wrong to assume that Hilda would be sitting at home waiting for him.

He took out the slip on which he had written down the name and address of the firm of accountants which Shayle had visited. Messrs Pomeroy, Ward & Pomeroy, of 88g The Strand, were in the telephone directory and he made a note of their number. Then he called the house of Sir Lancelot Anstey. He was remotely related to Anstey by marriage; Anstey managed all his legal affairs and, for a man of nearly seventy, viewed his activities with a remarkably benevolent eye.

When Anstey came to the telephone, he said:

'More trouble, Rolly?'

'Certainly not,' said Rollison. 'A trifling matter in which the advice of the most distinguished member of the legal profession would be welcome.'

Anstey chuckled.

'You certainly want me to do what I shouldn't!'

'If that were so I should come and see you with a bottle of fine old brandy,' said Rollison. 'The question before the oracle is—if you were not in existence, would anyone recommend me to take my business to Pomeroy, Ward & Pomeroy, of the Strand?'

'No,' said Anstey, promptly. 'Not unless they had a good reason to dislike you.'

'It's as bad as that, is it?'

'Now don't misunderstand me, Rolly,' said the older man. 'I know nothing against the firm, except that it sometimes handles cases which are rather unsavoury. It hasn't a large connection and it isn't very well-established. There is a companion firm of accountants— virtually the same people of course.'

'Is it a new firm?'

'It was started about ten years ago,' said Anstey. 'It specialises in raising loans and mortgages and arranges advances on testamentary expectations.

'Ah,' said Rollison. 'Money-lenders.'

'What makes you inquire?' said Anstey.

'You've probably heard of the case of the lady in high society who lost her memory,' said Rollison.

'Do Pomeroys claim to know her?'

'They haven't done, yet,' said Rollison. 'Many thanks for the information.'

'I suppose it's no use trying to make you explain,' said Anstey.

Although he had been very forthcoming for a lawyer, Anstey could probably have said much more. Rollison pondered over that and the record of the dual firms of Messrs Pomeroy, Ward & Pomeroy until the telephone awoke him from his reverie.

'Hallo, Jolly!' he said a moment later. 'News?'

'Of a kind, sir,' said Jolly. 'I am speaking from a telephone kiosk in the Strand. After making several brief calls at shops, and two telephone calls from public call-boxes, the young man returned to the office and is still there. I am now watching the entrance, sir, and it occurred to me that you would probably like to know at once what was happening.'

'Yes,' said Rollison. 'I'll come over at once. Follow him if he leaves again.'

'Very good, sir,' said Jolly.

Rollison picked up his hat and gloves and hurried downstairs. It was five minutes before he got a taxi but the driver made good speed and a quarter of an hour after he had received the message the taxi pulled up outside 80 The Strand. On the other side of the road, just emerging from an amusement hall from which came strident music, was Jolly. He showed himself for a moment and then disappeared.

Rollison paid the cabby and then went to 88g. On the ground floor there was a shop and at the side door a board with a list of those companies which had offices above. Pomeroy, Ward & Pomeroy occupied two name-plates and the whole of the second floor. He went up the stone stairs, unable to keep his progress quiet and so walking boldly.

There was only one door on the second floor landing, marked with the two firms' names and the word: *Inquiries.* A smaller hand-written notice invited everyone to '*Please Walk In.*'

Rollison did so.

He found himself in an empty outer office of sumptuous appearance. Here was nothing of the traditional fustiness of an accountant's or solicitor's office but chromium and light oak furniture, a thick pile carpet and a polished counter with a bell and the words: '*Please Ring If Office Empty.*' Comfortable armchairs with leather seats were lined along one wall and by the side of each was an ash-stand with a magazine rack. Rollison glanced at a dozen magazines and found they were current issues.

On the other side of the counter were three doors, one leading right and marked: 'Mr JE Pomeroy,' the others blank. From JE Pomeroy's office there came a murmur of conversation and, as Rollison lifted the flap in the counter and stepped through to the forbidden side, the clink of glasses. A man laughed, another spoke in a low-pitched voice which Rollison heard with difficulty and then the other man laughed more loudly. It was a throaty sound.

'Enjoying themselves,' murmured Rollison, and reached the door.

Suddenly the office was filled with the jangle of swing music which even a swing fan might have thought discordant. It came from Mr Pomeroy's office; the men inside were indeed about to enjoy themselves. The music was so loud that it was unlikely that they were carrying on a conversation. Rollison hesitated. If he opened the door and walked in, they might, with some justification, take a very high hand. He did not want to give them reasonable grounds for doing so and decided to return to the right side of the counter and ring the bell. As he turned, he saw a door opposite open.

He stood still.

'*Good* evening,' said Marcus Shayle.

He stood by the open door, smiling broadly, as if he were taking great pleasure in discomfiting Rollison, who stared at him without expression. Marcus Shayle *was* a man with most pleasant features. He had bright and rather merry eyes, his full lips smiled as if he were really amused and there was something boyish about his round face and curly hair. He was well-dressed in flannels and looked as flourishing as the outer office of the firm.

'Good evening,' said Rollison.

'Can I help you?' asked Shayle.

'I'm not sure,' said Rollison.

'Or would you prefer to help yourself?' asked Shayle, with a broad beam. 'I wonder if you will do something for me?'

It was clear that when Rollison had stepped through the counter he had trodden on a warning bell or a light—and that the radio had been switched on to deaden the sound of movement in the other room. The laughter was explained; it had been to deceive anyone who stood outside. In those few seconds his respect for Marcus Shayle and the firm rose considerably.

'Will you do something for me?' insisted Shayle.

'What?' asked Rollison, giving the impression that he was very much alarmed.

'Lift the telephone and dial Whitehall 1212,' said Shayle.

Rollison murmured: 'The number sounds familiar.'

'It's very well known,' said Shayle. 'You see, when a stranger forces open the door of this office and shows other indications of being here with a dishonest purpose, we *always* call the police.'

'Very sound policy,' said Rollison. 'The door was open.'

'Oh, I assure you that it was most securely locked.' Shayle stepped across to the door and put down the catch; as it clicked home, he laughed. 'You see? Only an extremely clever cracksman could pick that lock and the police will doubtless be able to identify you. You will oblige me, won't you?'

'I wonder if I should,' murmured Rollison.

'After all, if you were to try to get away or struggle or fight,' said Shayle, still in the best of good spirits, 'it would add violence to the crime.

'You could ring them yourself,' said Rollison.

'But that would spoil my enjoyment,' said Shayle. 'However, if you insist—'

'Oh, I'd hate to be disobliging,' said Rollison and he turned and lifted the receiver without batting an eye. Shayle looked startled. Deliberately Rollison dialled WHI 1212 with Shayle watching him closely so that he could be in no doubt about the number and he heard the operator at Scotland Yard.

'Give me Superintendent Grice, please,' he said.

The smile had faded completely from Shayle's face. He took a step forward and much of the pleasantness had gone, like his smile. In fact he looked disagreeably surprised and uncertain.

'I didn't tell you to ask for anyone,' he said.

'I know you would like to fly high,' murmured Rollison. '*Hallo?...* Oh, he's not in... No, I won't leave a message, unless—hold on a moment, will you?' He turned to Shayle and asked, politely: 'Would you like to leave a message?'

'No,' said Shayle, curtly.

'No, no message,' said Rollison and replaced the receiver. He took out his cigarette case and proffered it. Shayle waved it aside. He lit a cigarette, replaced the case and smiled. 'Checkmate,' he said. 'Or your move.'

'Who the devil are you?' demanded Shayle.

'I thought I was an expert cracksman,' said Rollison. 'Where do we go from here?'

'What do you want?' demanded Shayle.

'Freedom from fear for the fair sex,' murmured Rollison, and saw that the thrust reached home. 'Or—who put the poison in the *Neuro-Phosphates*? My dear chap, aren't you well?'

'What the devil are you talking about?' demanded Shayle. 'You have the nerve to break into this office and to start uttering threats—'

'No threats meant, only taken,' smiled Rollison. 'We aren't getting very far, are we? May I see who's with you?'

'Get out of here!' snapped Shayle.

'After all,' said Rollison, reasoningly, 'I'm only looking for a pair of painter's overalls with a large gun-pocket and that's the kind of thing I might find anywhere.'

'I haven't the faintest idea what you mean!'

'Then let's make ourselves comfortable and I'll tell you a story,' said Rollison. He stepped to the door of Pomeroy's room and, before Shayle could stop him, thrust it open. It struck an obstruction on the other side and swung back against Rollison's hand but he was ready for it and thrust it open again. Into the middle of the office a man was staggering back, a little round podge of a man who held his plump right hand to his face and whose eyes were watering freely. He wore a remarkable suit of red, yellow and white check and looked a very sporting gentleman.

'Mr Pomeroy, I presume,' murmured Rollison.

Mr Pomeroy, if it were he, was bereft of words. He took a colourful handkerchief from his pocket and dabbed gingerly at his nose while Shayle strode forward and clapped a hand on Rollison's shoulder with the manifest intention of swinging him round and throwing him out of the office. Rollison steeled himself so that Shayle could not move him and looked into the eyes which were no longer merry but blazing with anger.

Rollison slipped from Shayle's hold without trouble, eyed the men thoughtfully and noted the bright red spots on the coloured handkerchief; the sporting gentleman's weak feature was obviously his nose.

Neither of the others spoke.

'The fount of words dries up,' said Rollison. 'Perhaps that's just as well. Listen to me with great care. I have a reputation for liking the ladies and on my visiting list at the moment are two; Miss Phyllis Armitage and the forlorn one at the Lawley Nursing Home. I should hate anything to happen to either of them. As a matter of fact there are three, for there is Miss Armitage's younger sister. Do I make myself clear?'

CHAPTER SEVEN

September The Thirtieth

THE SPORTING GENTLEMAN appeared to be solely concerned with his nose, although now and again he shot a quick, birdlike glance at Rollison. Neither of them spoke and Rollison judged it the right moment to withdraw. He did not think the police would be long in arriving and they would probably hold Shayle for questioning.

'I hope you'll remember,' he said.

Shayle took a step forward, as if to prevent him from leaving, but changed his mind. The other stopped dabbing his nose and glared at him. It was a peculiar glare. Most people would have thought the fat man a witless creature of no account but his expression was not far removed from malignance.

Rollison went into the outer office, closing the door behind him. He stepped across to the passage and hurried down the steps.

He hoped to find Grice coming along the road but there was no sign of the Wolseley. He walked across the road to the amusement hall from whence the strident cacophony was apparently affording amusement to a small crowd gathered at the entrance. Near the door were glass-enclosed machines filled with tiny glass balls with which were mixed a variety of glittering articles, apparently of great value. For sixpence one could pull a handle which operated a small crane and disport oneself trying to get a glittering article between the claws and so win it as a prize. At the far end of the hall was a rifle range and clay pipes and pigeons, round the walls were a remarkable variety of machines, all patronised and all offering something for nothing in a game of skill which certainly skilfully avoided the gaming laws. From the depth of the hall came warm, rather smelly air as well as the noises of machines and men and women, the clink of coins and the jovial, congratulatory voice of an attendant when a player won a prize.

There was no sign of Jolly.

He had stationed himself at one of the machines near the door to get a better view of 88g The Strand and Rollison had expected to find him still there. He stood near the entrance, pretending to watch the fun and games and actually looking for Grice's car. It did not come.

After a quarter of an hour the fat little man came out of the doorway, looked rather nervously in each direction and then hailed a taxi. A stream of traffic prevented Rollison from crossing the road quickly and the taxi was out of sight, going towards Trafalgar Square, before he could get another cab. Grimly, Rollison resigned himself to waiting for Shayle.

At last Grice arrived.

Rollison watched the Superintendent get out and hurry into the building accompanied by two sergeants. He expected them to be some time and to come out with Shayle. They were less than ten minutes and they came out without him. Rollison overcame the temptation to show his presence and watched Grice drive away. Obviously Shayle had made his way out by a back entrance. He dallied with the idea of making a quick search of the offices, decided against it and walked through the gathering dusk towards Piccadilly.

In the affair so far there were all the makings of discord with the police.

A light was shining from the window of his living-room and, as he walked towards the house, he saw Jolly drawing the curtains. That was more cheering and he hurried up the stairs, let himself in with a key and met Jolly coming out of the bedroom.

'Did the Fun Fair make you tired?' There was an unusual edge to Rollison's voice.

'No, sir,' said Jolly, 'I thought it wise to leave when faced with the need for making a quick decision without being able to consult you.'

'Oh,' said Rollison.

'Some five minutes after you went into the building, sir,' said Jolly, with great deliberation, 'Miss Gwendoline Barrington-Ley arrived.' His expression did not change when he saw Rollison's astonishment. 'I was greatly interested, of course, and somewhat surprised when she came out after a very few minutes and walked back towards Trafalgar Square. I thought it wise to follow her and was somewhat disappointed when she returned, on foot, to Barrington House. I thought it better to return here.'

'Quite rightly,' said Rollison. 'Get me a drink, Jolly.'

'Whisky, sir?'

'Yes. Don't spare the soda.'

Rollison sat down and watched his man get the drink from a chiffonier of great age which vandals said was now a cocktail cabinet. He took the glass and drank slowly. Jolly hovered in the background for some minutes and then walked towards the door.

'Don't go,' said Rollison.

'Very good, sir.' Jolly went over to the book-cases in the corner of the room and appeared to interest himself in straightening the books on the shelves. After a long silence, Rollison spoke as if to himself:

'That suggests that she did not tell me all the truth, doesn't it?'

'A possibility which you had already considered, sir.'

'And which I hoped wouldn't be substantiated,' said Rollison. 'Jolly, I am not covering myself with glory. I've prevented Grice from catching Marcus Shayle—your pleasant young man. And how pleasant!' Rollison finished his whisky, lit a cigarette and began to talk, going over everything that had happened in a matter-of-fact voice, as if he were anxious to get it all clear in his own mind.

Jolly did not interrupt. He showed some concern when he heard of the poisoning and of the man with the gun and, when at last Rollison finished, he said:

'You appear to have been instrumental in saving Miss Armitage from injury, sir, and you may have been just in time to save the unknown lady.'

'No credit where no credit's due,' said Rollison. 'The matron was telephoning the doctor and that was not because I was on the spot. The unknown lady—what shall we call her?'

After a moment, Jolly suggested: 'Lady Lost, sir?'

'I suppose that's as good as anything,' said Rollison. 'Where was I?' He went on with hardly a pause. 'Lady Lost was in no great danger; obviously the poison was not enough to kill her. I think my painter would have shot Phyllis Armitage but, now that these people know that the police have visited Messrs Pomeroy, Ward & Pomeroy, she will probably be all right. It isn't often that a man thinks it worth taking a pot-shot at someone who *might* be able to give evidence against him.' He paused. 'Well, I want to know who sent me that photograph. I think I'll have a snack and then go to Barrington House.'

'I will prepare something for you at once,' said Jolly.

Rollison dialled Whitehall 1212, only to learn that Grice had left for home. He tried the Chelsea number, and was answered by the Superintendent.

'Why the devil didn't you tell me that the girl had given you Shayle's name?' demanded Grice. 'You try one's patience beyond endurance. You went to see Shayle, didn't you?'

'Yes,' said Rollison.

'You're never happy unless you think you're one step ahead of us,' complained Grice. 'Did you see Shayle?'

'I'm afraid so,' said Rollison, apologetically.

'I suppose you know you scared him away?'

'Late arrival of the police is hardly a fault of mine,' murmured Rollison. 'In any case, Shayle caught me on the wrong foot. While I was in his office I telephoned the Yard. You weren't there.'

'Then why didn't you wait until I arrived?'

'I did,' said Rollison. 'Shayle went out the back way.'

'Was he there alone?'

'No,' said Rollison. He told Grice about the gentleman in sporting tweeds and mentioned that because his nose had come in contact with the door it might be red and swollen. By the time the conversation was over and Jolly had come in with a tray on which was an omelette, Grice was mollified though obviously not pleased. He assured Rollison that Phyllis Armitage would be watched, not only because she might not have told the whole truth but because she might be in personal danger. At least, thought Rollison, he accepted the theory that the pseudo-painter had meant to prevent her from talking.

Rollison sat down and began to eat and then said:

'There is a snag about Shayle—have you seen it, Jolly?'

'Not yet, sir.'

'Shayle wanted Phyllis Armitage to go back on duty. Would he have worried about that if Lady Lost had been dead—or if he thought she would die? Why did he try to poison her and then show such anxiety about her well-being? Why did he get the nurse out of the room when, later, he wanted her to report to him anything that Lady Lost said?'

'I see, sir,' said Jolly.

'Contradictory motives,' remarked Rollison.

He continued to eat, making an occasional comment. Jolly interpolated a word now and again but did nothing to brighten his spirits. A little before half-past nine Rollison left for Barrington House. Lights were shining through gaps in the curtains as he entered the garden. There was a wait of some minutes after he had rung the bell and then a footman opened the door—the man who had been on duty that morning. He recognised Rollison on sight.

'Good evening, sir.'

'I'm a little late,' said Rollison. 'Is Mrs Barrington-Ley at home?'

'I believe so, sir. If you will wait just one moment, I will make sure.'

The footman went off, and as Rollison waited in the hall he had an uncomfortable feeling that he was being watched. While showing great interest in an oil-painting which he did not admire, he looked about him. There were several closed doors and only one, on the first landing, which was ajar. A light was coming from it and there was a shadow on the wall nearby. Rollison turned towards the opposite wall and, after a moment, swung round quickly.

Outlined in the doorway was the round face of the sporting gentleman, his nose very swollen!

The man closed the door quickly. Rollison moved slowly towards the stairs but before he reached them the footman came from a downstairs room and announced that Mrs Barrington-Ley would see him.

'Thanks,' Rollison said. 'Who is the gentleman in draught-board tweeds?'

'I *beg* your pardon, sir?'

'The man I saw upstairs just now,' said Rollison.

He thought that the man was going to be evasive but the fellow changed his mind and said:

'Perhaps you mean Mr Pomeroy, sir.'

'Has he a right to be here?'

The footman stared. 'Naturally, sir, or he wouldn't be here. Perhaps you would like to inquire from Mrs Barrington-Ley?'

There was an undercurrent of insolence in the man's manner, reminding Rollison of his earlier doubts. He nodded and walked to the door of the sitting-room.

Hilda Barrington-Ley rose quickly from an easy chair and approached him with hands outstretched. She was a demonstrative little creature for whom most of her friends had much affection. She

wore an evening gown of midnight blue satin in which she looked
chic and attractive—and, thought Rollison, she was trying hard to
pretend that she had nothing on her mind.

'Why, Rolly, how delightful!'

'The word is beautiful,' smiled Rollison, taking her hands. 'You
ought to be prostrate after the ball and instead you look as if you want
to compete with the morning dew. How are you?'

'*Very* pleased,' said Hilda. 'We made nearly six thousand pounds
for charity, Rolly, isn't it magnificent? I do wish you had been there
but how sweet of you to send a cheque. *Do* sit down. What will you
have to drink?'

'Nothing, thanks.'

'Oh, you must!' She fluttered to a table where there were decanters,
bottles and glasses which shone in the light from an electric chandelier.
'*I* feel like champagne,' she said, 'but I don't suppose you do. Whisky
or brandy?'

Rollison laughed. 'Whisky, thanks. You're very bright.'

'Haven't I every reason to *be* bright?' she demanded.

'I suppose so. Hilda—' He stepped to her side and watched her
handle the decanter, the rings on her small, white hands glittering,
everything about her light and lively and lovely. She deliberately
ignored the more sober note in his voice as he went on: 'Who is
Pomeroy?'

'Pomeroy?' echoed Hilda. Her hand tightened on the glass but she
had herself under control and looked at him brightly. 'Oh, that funny
little fat man. He's come to see David. Isn't he sweet?'

'Why does he want to see David?' demanded Rollison.

'*I* don't know,' said Hilda. 'Is that as you like it?' She handed him
his glass and looked him squarely in the eyes. 'I never interfere with
anything David does. Finance is absolutely *beyond* me, Rolly.
Cheers!'

'Cheers,' said Rollison and sipped his drink. 'Is David in?'

'No, he's not,' said Hilda. 'But you know what it is like these
days—loans for Africa, loans for India, loans for every country which
needs them; he's so busy, poor dear, that he hardly ever gets in early.
Oh! If you're thinking of Mr Pomeroy, he's waiting for David—he
said he would wait until half-past ten and I didn't like to refuse him,

although goodness knows when David will come back. Is that all right?'

'I can't interfere,' said Rollison, deliberately obtuse.

'I mean the whisky?'

'Oh, yes, thanks.' Rollison followed her as she walked to a chair and sat down. He had not suspected Hilda of such ability to dissemble. She was worried but determined not to admit it. 'How is the lady of the lost memory?' he asked, casually.

'Poor thing, she's had a relapse,' said Hilda, brightly. 'I was hoping she would be able to come here for a few days but she isn't likely to be released from the nursing home for a week. Perhaps she'll have recovered her memory by then. Wasn't it a strange business?'

'Very.'

'No one seems to know her,' said Hilda. 'After the story in the newspaper I quite thought a lot of people would prove they had seen her before. A few *have* claimed to know her; a policeman was here a little while ago and he told me so but he said they were just seeking publicity. *Don't* people do strange things?'

'Very strange,' agreed Rollison.

'But then, you're an expert on odd happenings, aren't you?' said Hilda. She put down her glass. 'Why, Rolly! Perhaps *you* can help her!'

'What makes you say that?' asked Rollison, a little heavily.

'Why, it's a mystery, isn't it?' asked Hilda, eagerly. 'It's exactly the kind of thing that interests you—I'll introduce her to you when she's a little better. Will you have another?'

'No, thanks,' said Rollison. 'And I ought to be going.'

'What, so soon?' Her voice suggested that she wanted him to stay but she stood up promptly. 'Do come again when you can spare a few minutes, Rolly, and if you are interested in my lost lady, that would be splendid!'

Rollison found himself in the hall with Hilda chattering all the time. The footman appeared from a doorway and opened the door. Hilda repeated how delighted she was that he had called and how she hoped that he would come again soon—and then Rollison found himself on the porch with the door closed firmly behind him and a feeling of great disquiet in his mind.

*   *   *

The disquiet continued.

The lost lady did not die and the doctors said that she would be able to leave the nursing home by the end of the month. There were no further attempts to attack her. Phyllis Armitage resigned from her post and, as far as the police and Rollison were able to find out, did not seek other work. Her sister came to stay with her at the flatlet.

On the day after Rollison's burst of activity, Grice went to the offices of Pomeroy, Ward & Pomeroy. The two firms were in many respects as one and had the same principals. Grice was received by a pompous, well-dressed gentleman who denied all knowledge of the sporting gent but admitted that Marcus Shayle was his head clerk. Shayle had not come to the office that morning.

He did not come to the office that afternoon, nor on the following days. The police found no trace either of him or the man in coloured check tweeds. Messrs Pomeroy, Ward & Pomeroy, Grice told Rollison, were very correct in their behaviour and professed to be puzzled by the disappearance of their head clerk.

The Barrington-Leys left London for their Sussex home. On the two occasions when Rollison tried to get in touch with Gwendoline, he failed—and obviously she meant him to fail.

In all, thirty-five people wrote to Scotland Yard or called there in person, declaring that they had recognised the photograph in *The Record*. The lost lady was variously described as a Pole, a Czech, a Russian, a Greek and a French Countess, the wife of a grocer's assistant, a school-mistress, a spiritualist medium, an obscure musical comedy star, the winner of a beauty competition a few years ago and other things but none of the claims could be substantiated. The only two people who gained the ear of the police could not name her but said that they had seen her in a small restaurant in Soho where she had dined in a secluded corner on three successive nights before her appearance at Barrington House. Grice went himself to see the proprietor and arrived when the lady in question was in her secluded corner, vaguely like the woman of the photograph; she was a mannequin at a West End store.

'It *can't* just peter out,' said Rollison, glumly.

He tried to find out what loans Barrington-Ley was financing but no one in the City was able to give him reliable information. There was a vague rumour that Barrington-Ley was not well but there were no open suggestions that his finances were in bad order. Friends had advised him to rest, which was why he was out of London, but he visited the City two or three times a week and maintained a regular correspondence with his office.

Then dawned the thirtieth of September.

Never had Jolly known Rollison in such poor spirits over so long a period. Seldom had he spent so many evenings at home, renewing, he said, his acquaintance with the older poets but often sitting with a book open in his hands and obviously pondering over more recent matters. On the twenty-ninth of September Jolly, almost distraught, clung to the hope that a regimental dinner would cheer him up. It did—and, walking along the wide passage of the officer's club he saw Grice.

'Great Scott!' he said. 'Have you joined the Army?'

'Where is she?' demanded Grice, sharply.

'Who?' inquired Rollison.

'Rolly, you've gone too far this time. Where is that woman?'

'Which woman?' asked Rollison but the smile left his face and his mind flew to the unconscious woman of the pale face and the lacklustre eyes.

Grice, who was breathing rather heavily, rested a hand on his arm. Only a serious matter would have made him brave the lion's den and go through the obstructionist ceremony which all without a special pass were compelled to endure downstairs.

'The woman has disappeared from the nursing home,' he said with great care. 'The matron says that she had a letter from you and within an hour she had gone. She dressed in the evening gown in which she was first found, as she had no others. She wasn't fit enough to travel far. Where have you taken her?'

Rollison said: 'Is the nursing home watched?'

'That's nothing to do with it.'

'It's a lot to do with it,' said Rollison. 'If it were watched your men either fell down on the job or else she went out dressed very different from what you say. Had you a man on duty?'

'Two,' said Grice.

'Then probably she didn't go out in an evening gown,' said Rollison, hurrying along the passage with a hand on Grice's arm, 'and she certainly didn't get a letter from me.'

'She did,' said Grice. 'I've seen it.'

CHAPTER EIGHT

The Toff Has A Visitor

THE LETTER, WHICH was soon established as a forgery, said so little that Grice admitted that there was no real reason for thinking that it explained the woman's disappearance. In fact as they went to Grice's office, Rollison came to the conclusion that the Superintendent had never been really convinced that he was behind it but had drawn a bow at a venture.

The letter said that Rollison knew the woman's identity.

Grice said: 'Do you?'

'No,' said Rollison.

'You haven't sat back and counted chickens this last three weeks, have you?'

'I've got no practical results,' said Rollison. 'Have you?'

'None at all,' admitted Grice. He sat back, worriedly. 'I know no more about her now than I did when she first appeared but at least one attempt has been made to murder her and I am afraid of what might happen next. We might find her body. Why were you so interested in the Barrington-Leys?'

'Because she turned up at their house.'

'You know the family well, don't you?'

'Fairly well.'

'Why did they suddenly leave London?'

'I haven't a notion.'

'The daughter came to see you on the day you first heard of the affair, didn't she?'

'Yes.'

'What about?'

'I don't see why this interests you,' said Rollison, 'but she came because she didn't want her mother to dispense charity on this woman. She thought I might be able to say enough to discredit Lady Lost.'

'That's pretty thin,' said Grice. He leaned forward. 'Rolly, there are times when personal loyalty has no place in one's actions. If you are hiding, or trying to hide, anything about the Barrington-Leys, you are making a big mistake.' He paused, then asked tersely: 'Is Barrington-Ley in difficulties?'

'Not to my knowledge,' said Rollison.

'Did you know that they've recently used Pomeroy, Ward & Pomeroy for most of their audit work?'

'Yes,' said Rollison.

'Then why the devil didn't you tell me?'

'I thought it was general knowledge to the police if not to the public.'

'I doubt that,' said Grice, still bad tempered, 'but I suppose I'll have to accept your word for it.' He stood up. 'Rolly, we've worked together a lot and I've always given you your head when I could. I hope you won't let me down this time. You know something more than you admit, don't you?'

'Nothing that even remotely concerns the police,' said Rollison. 'I have told you of the little fat man who was with Marcus Shayle—have you traced him yet?'

'No,' said Grice, sourly, 'although I think he *is* a Pomeroy. The principals aren't too happy about him.'

'Find him and Shayle, instead of leathering me,' said Rollison and rose to go.

He did not like being on strained terms with Grice and was not sure that he was justified in respecting Gwendoline's confidence. The rumours about Barrington-Ley's financial position had not yet reached him but if they materialised he would have to tell Grice of Gwendoline's suspicions. On the other hand, Grice might have invented these rumours to try to make him talk.

As Rollison saw the position, there was a possibility that the root cause was a domestic upset in the family.

He went to Gresham Terrace, still troubled but much more alert than he had been for days. Grice might be right in his fears for the lost lady's life and he could not get out of his mind the fact that Marcus Shayle had wanted to know what she said while she was unconscious. The contradictory motives puzzled him most.

As he inserted his key in the lock, the door opened—a sure sign that Jolly did not want it known that he had returned. He entered, without speaking, and Jolly closed the door without a sound. Voices came from the living-room—the first a woman's voice which startled him.

'Miss Armitage has called, sir,' whispered Jolly, 'with her sister.'

'Have they said what they want?' asked Rollison.

'Not freely, sir. They have, however, been quarrelling since they arrived. I have heard an occasional word and I thought you might like to play upon their differences of opinion.

Both girls were sitting down when he entered the room and both looked eagerly towards him. The first thing that struck him about Janice Armitage was her youthfulness; she looked no more than sixteen or seventeen. The second thing was her clothes; she was extremely well-dressed—far better than her sister. She wore a dark green coat and a dress of the same material, the coat trimmed with sable. There was something comical about her face. It was round and she had the snub nose which seemed to run in the family but none of Phyllis's prettiness or air of perpetual surprise. She had very round eyes, a wrinkled forehead and a petulant mouth.

'Why, hallo!' said Rollison, as if greeting old friends, 'how nice to see you!' He shook hands first with Janice who looked taken aback. 'Phyllis, you deceived me, you didn't tell me how attractive your sister was!' He stood back, still holding the younger girl's hand, admiration in his eyes—and she fell for it as if she had never had a compliment in her life.

'Why, hello,' she said, in a voice of exaggerated refinement. 'I've *so* wanted to meet you, Mr Rollison.'

'If I'd known the truth I would have wanted to meet you,' said Rollison. He turned to Phyllis and took her hand—and winked. The expression of amazement on her face faded and she hid a smile. 'Now, isn't it time for a drink?'

'I don't—' began Phyllis.

'Don't take any notice of Phyllis,' said Janice, with a *moue*, 'she's a sober old stick. I'd love a gin-and-It.'

Rollison went to the wall and pressed the bell, although he was quite sure that Jolly was standing near the door. After a discreet pause, Jolly entered. Rollison imagined that the younger girl would get a kick out of having the drinks served by Jolly and, as she preened herself and tucked a few odd strands into the regimented waves of her hair, he knew that he was right to butter Janice Armitage excessively.

'And you?' he asked Phyllis.

'I'd rather not,' said Phyllis, and then relented. 'Well, perhaps a sherry.'

'Dry or sweet?'

'Dry, please,' she said and Rollison beamed at Janice and said that he would follow her example. He watched Jolly's impassive face as the drinks were poured. Then Jolly retired and Rollison drank to his guests. Janice made it clear that she was mostly pleasantly surprised.

'I don't know why Phyllis wanted me to come,' she said, 'and I don't mind admitting that at first I didn't want to—not a bit. I don't often get on with friends of Phyllis's. You're different, though I don't know where on earth she met you.'

Rollison smiled. 'We can't tell you all our secrets.'

'Oh, go on,' said Janice.

'It doesn't matter,' said Phyllis. 'Mr Rollison, I told you that Janice was engaged to Marcus Shayle, didn't I?'

'What does that matter—I'm not now,' said Janice, tartly. 'There's no need to bring that up.'

'There is,' said Phyllis, wearily. 'You've been hearing from him.'

'I tell you I haven't! And it's no business of yours if I have and I certainly don't see why it should concern Mr Rollison. A girl can have a letter now and again, can't she?'

'Marcus Shayle,' murmured Rollison, 'is wanted by the police. Don't you know that?'

'Well, *I* don't know where he is,' said Janice, 'and I certainly don't think Marcus would do anything wrong; the police are fools, everyone knows that. It's really too bad!' she went on, raising her voice, 'you didn't say you were going to talk about this with Mr Rollison, he doesn't want to hear—do you?'

'Only if you can tell me where to find Shayle,' said Rollison, improvising magnificently. 'You see, he once let a friend of mine down rather badly and I'd like a few words with the gentleman. Still, if you don't know where he is—' He paused, invitingly, and Janice jumped in.

'I certainly don't! And I am *not* receiving presents from him. I don't have to explain to Phyllis every time I have a new dress, do I?'

Phyllis's expression told Rollison that he now knew the whole purport of the call. So he sympathised a little with Janice and said that he was sure she deserved every present she received. Janice, elated at scoring a triumph over her sister, grew more and more fulsome and drank more and more gin-and-Italians. Phyllis sat back with a look of hopeless resignation.

Finally it transpired that Janice was receiving letters from Marcus Shayle, letters with a Devon address—an address where Janice had once been to see him. Everything was very proper, of course, and after all they had been engaged, hadn't they? She was nearly drunk by then and grew a little maudlin while Phyllis sat back, disapproving and, Rollison thought, angry and hurt by the exhibition which her sister was making of herself.

Then Janice wanted to powder her nose.

Jolly escorted her with great dignity to the bathroom, leaving Rollison free for a word with her sister. Phyllis got up quickly, and said:

'I knew she was hearing from him and that he was sending her money. I couldn't make her tell me where he is but I thought you might. I have done right, haven't I?'

'Perfectly, in more ways than one, but let's change the subject— have you seen the patient again?'

'No,' said Phyllis, startled. 'Isn't she still at the nursing home?'

'They say that she made a voluntary departure,' said Rollison. 'Do you know whether Marcus Shayle has anything to do with the nursing home?'

'No.'

'Have you ever seen him in the company of a fat man with a nice taste in broad checks?'

'No,' said Phyllis, 'but Janice knows him much better than I do.'

Janice was more dignified on her return and Rollison decided not to press the inquiry about the little fat man. He made an appointment with Janice for the next day, for lunch, and then ushered them out. When they had gone, Rollison drew his hand across his forehead and became aware of Jolly standing at his side.

'Two very different beans out of the same pod,' said Jolly, gravely.

Rollison laughed. 'Very different is right.'

'Are we going to Devonshire, sir?' asked Jolly.

'Not yet,' said Rollison, 'but we are going to cheer Grice up. If Shayle's at the Devon address the police will get him before the night's out.' He went to the telephone and tried Grice's home number.

'How much is Shayle's address worth?' Rollison asked.

'What?' cried Grice. 'Have you got it?'

Rollison passed on the necessary particulars. The Superintendent was in such a hurry to get in touch with the Devonshire police that he did not even ask Rollison where he had obtained the information but rang off and said that he would look in later. Rollison replaced the receiver, paused for a moment, and then said slowly: 'Jolly.'

'Yes, sir.'

'If she is alive, I am going to find Lady Lost.'

'I am sure you are sir,' said Jolly, 'I have no doubt at all about that. I—excuse me.'

He made his dignified way towards the hall and the front door, for the bell had rung. Before he opened it there was another ring which did not stop until there was an exclamation from Jolly—one so unexpected and so out of character that Rollison was afraid his man had been hurt. He stepped swiftly to the door, putting his right hand to his pocket, an instinctive gesture for he was not carrying a gun.

Before he looked round the door, some of his fears were dispelled, for Jolly said in a voice that was a little unsteady:

'Good evening, Madam.'

Rollison stepped forward—and he saw Lady Lost huddled in costly furs, bare-headed and very pale, push past Jolly and walk slowly towards him.

CHAPTER NINE

'Come Back Peter, Fly Away Paul'

ON THE WOMAN'S lips was a smile which made her the living image of that photograph; as indeed, she was. She advanced slowly towards Rollison, her right hand outstretched, and he stood still. The photograph had been a triumph of the camera's art but beside this woman it was insignificant, a dull shadow, a paltry thing to be forgotten.

Her eyes were hazel, the brown lashes curled upwards as if nature had been improved upon and yet Rollison got the impression that their curve was natural. Her eyes slanted ever so little towards the temples and her cheek-bones *were* high although not remarkably so; certainly the type was not English. But what most attracted him was her complexion. There was not a tinge of colour in it; it was like alabaster, pale and glowing, so perfect that it did not seem quite real. She had used no make-up and her lips were only faintly outlined yet, in spite of that, warmth and vitality seemed to spring from her.

When he touched her outstretched hand and bowed over it, her fingers were cool.

'You are very welcome,' he murmured and into his eyes there sprang a smile, at once gallant and gay. When Jolly saw it, his own face lit up; here was the real Rollison.

'You are very kind,' said the woman.

Her voice had a huskiness which was attractive. There was a trace of foreign accent, too.

'After all,' said Rollison, taking her arm and leading her into the study, 'I've been wanting to talk to you for a long time.'

'So I understand,' she said. 'You wrote to me.'

Rollison did not correct her.

'And you lied to me,' she said slowly. 'I can see that now—you have never seen me before and you do not know who I am, although in your letter you said you did.' Something of her vitality seemed to ebb and she sat down slowly. Rollison took her coat and handed it to Jolly.

She looked up at him. 'Why did you make me hope?'

'Not I,' said Rollison, 'but a mutual friend. I'm glad that he wrote to you, because otherwise you would not have come.'

She frowned. '*More* knavery?' The word came naturally from her lips.

'More knavery which we can counter,' said Rollison, sitting on the arm of his chair and smiling at her. 'Will you have a drink?'

She said: 'No, but I am very hungry.'

'That can soon be put right,' said Rollison and he rang for Jolly. 'We will have dinner as quickly as possible.'

'Very good, sir.' Jolly retired and Rollison looked back at the woman.

If she were not lying by inference, her memory was no better than when she had arrived at Barrington House. It was too soon for him to be convinced that she was telling the truth and yet he wanted to believe her. From the moment he had seen her photograph he had wanted to see her in the flesh, to hear her voice and see the colour of her eyes, to know the living reality of her—and here she was, dressed in a plain black evening gown with shoes of black satin trimmed with *diamanté*, without other jewellery or make-up, with her brown hair plaited and coiled about her head and shining with a soft lustre.

'So,' she said, speaking with great deliberation, 'you do not know me and you cannot help me.'

'Only the first is true,' he said.

She looked puzzled. 'Why should that be?'

'Nearly a month ago, before you arrived at Barrington House, an unknown person sent me your photograph and I have been at your command from that moment!'

She smiled. 'An Englishman who is gallant!'

'There is more in us than you suspect,' he said. 'So you know that you are not English?'

'That is one thing about which there is no doubt,' she said.

'The doctors were quite sure of that and so they tried to make me remember what I am and yet they failed. I remember *nothing*, except appearing in that gay ballroom with many strange people looking at me. Then the room suddenly began to go round, the lights danced, the people swayed as they came towards me—and then, darkness!' Throughout that speech her voice had been pitched on so low a key that he could hear what she said only with difficulty. After a long while, she went on: 'Darkness and the hospital and all that happened afterwards. I remember quite well.'

'Everything?' asked Rollison.

'Everything,' she said, 'and yet not enough, for your police have asked me whether I saw a stranger in my room and I remember no stranger; I remember only that I was sick, so very sick and I did not think that I would live. Yet I am here—as I was there—seeking *myself.*'

'With others also looking for you,' said Rollison. 'Someone knows who you are.'

Her eyes lit up. 'That is the first time I have been given real hope! Can you be sure?'

'Quite sure,' said Rollison. 'They would not be so interested in you unless they knew who you were and what you are doing in England.' He remembered himself and offered her cigarettes but she refused and also refused another offer of a drink. So he went on: 'What they know, we can learn, and when we've learned it then the doctors can help you to remember all that you've forgotten.'

'Almost you make it sound simple.'

'Few things are as complicated as they look,' said Rollison. 'I wonder if the doctors or the police realise one thing that can be helpful?'

'What do you mean?'

'That you learned English in England or from an English governess with whom you spoke the language from childhood,' said Rollison. 'Have they said that?'

'No. You are performing miracles, Mr Rollison! I am already becoming excited.'

'After dinner you will probably get hilarious,' said Rollison, for he heard Jolly coming into the hall. 'Now, you *must* have some sherry.'

'I do not like it,' she said.

He stared down at her, leaning forward a little, his eyes brighter than ever.

'You see! Another thing you remember.'

'But—'

'They don't give you sherry in the nursing home,' said Rollison, 'so you must have disliked it before you lost your memory. A cocktail?'

She made a face. 'They burn one so!' Her eyes lighted up, not with the effort of remembering but because some things were coming to her mind so naturally. 'There are two things I do not like about the Americans—they invented cocktails and they invented high buildings.'

'Which are called?'

She stared at him with great concentration and then said delightedly: 'Sky-scrapers!'

'Sky-scrapers,' echoed Rollison. He was surprised by his own elation.

Jolly came in and laid the table while they talked gaily and irresponsibly and for the first time a tinge of colour crept into her cheeks. As they talked, he recalled all that he had heard about her. When she had arrived at Barrington House she had no jewellery, no handbag, no papers, nothing but the clothes in which she now stood: clothes which Grice had told him were of American make and could not be traced in England. According to the police no one could be sure who had made her gown or who had supplied her furs.

Marcus Shayle had wanted to know what she said. He or some unknown person had tried to kill her. Another had sent her the letter which had brought her here.

'You have thought of something else,' she said, seeing the gleam in his eyes.

'Yes,' said Rollison. 'That letter. Whoever sent it wanted you to come here and the man or woman who sent me your photograph also wanted me to meet you. So they were probably sent by the same person.'

'It is most likely,' she said.

Jolly had been busy with steaks and frozen peas and grilled tomatoes and murmured that dinner was served. He hovered about them throughout the meal while they talked and laughed with animation; this was a miracle. They drank sparingly of champagne, but enough to bring an added sparkle to their eyes, and behaved as if they were old friends who had met after a long separation. No stranger would have believed that they had met for the first time only an hour before.

She would have coffee, she said.

She grimaced when she sipped it and set her cup down without taking it up again. Rollison noticed that and made no comment. Then being a woman, she rose and looked at herself in a small mirror, and exclaimed in mock horror.

'Mr Rollison, I am—'

'Delightful,' he said.

'But my lips! And my cheeks! I am like a ghost!'

'A very lively ghost,' said Rollison. 'Come with me.' He took her to the dressing-table where, spread out, was everything any woman could need for her make-up and her toilet; Jolly had found time to put them ready. She sat at the dressing-table, looking up at him, and he went out and closed the door.

Jolly was clearing the table.

'We're getting results,' said Rollison, his voice much more confident. 'Get that cleared as quickly as you can and then—Jolly.'

'Yes, sir.'

'Who has the best collection of gramophone records of our acquaintance?'

Jolly considered. 'Mr Jeffrey, sir, or perhaps Sir Lancelot Anstey.'

'Sir Lancelot—he's the man! Go and borrow some records from him. We want the Yugoslav National Anthem—in fact the National Anthems of all the Balkan countries—some national music from them all, folk-songs, gypsy music, a good general selection. If Sir Lancelot hasn't got them he will know where to find them at short notice and I want them to-night.'

'I will obtain them, sir,' said Jolly, confidently.

'And Jolly, there is a curious, syrupy, bitter stuff which the Turks and some others call coffee. Have you ever made it?'

'I am afraid not, sir, but I believe that it is obtainable at several small restaurants. Shall I endeavour to obtain some of that also?'

'Yes. Don't lose time, Jolly, but don't take chances. She was probably followed here.'

'I have thought of that, sir.'

'If she were followed here it was by a friend; an enemy would not have let her come. So deal lightly with anyone you suspect.'

Rollison went to the telephone and he dialled Grice's home number again. This time he was unlucky; for Grice was at the Yard. He had him on the wire very soon and it was a jubilant Grice—a fact which puzzled Rollison, who had forgotten a great deal since the arrival of "the lady."

'I was going to come round to see you, Rolly,' said Grice. 'I'll take back most of what I've said about you.'

'Why?' asked Rollison.

'We've got Marcus Shayle,' said Grice. 'The Devon police have just telephoned me—he was at the address you gave me.'

'Now you know my value,' said Rollison. 'Was anyone else with him?'

'No, he was alone.'

'A pity but it's progress,' said Rollison. 'Now, a Roland for your Oliver—I have the lady here.'

After a long pause, Grice asked: '*What* did you say?'

'In the flesh,' said Rollison, 'and we're getting along famously. I hope you won't interrupt us yet. I'll see that she is all right and I'll get some incurious relative to spend the night here, unless—I say, old chap.'

'Er—yes,' said Grice, still taken aback.

'Have you a good woman detective who can play the part of a maid?'

'Yes,' said Grice, promptly.

'Send her over, will you,' said Rollison and Grice, still elated by the capture of Marcus Shayle, promised that he would.

Rollison rang off and looked towards the bedroom door. He did not think that his guest would be much longer; she had been there nearly a quarter of an hour. Jolly had gone and the flat was very quiet. He lit a cigarette and smiled to himself, letting the mystifying development take second place in his enjoyment of the situation. He took the photograph from his desk and propped it up against the wall. Then, just as he was about to knock at the bedroom door, the ringing of the telephone bell sounded very loud. He answered it and said 'Hallo'. A confused murmuring reached his ears, low-pitched and rather breathless voices which, he thought, belonged to women. He expected it to be a call from Phyllis or Janice Armitage and that they were perhaps in a call-box together.

'Hallo,' he repeated, 'this is Mayfair —'

'*Rolly*!' exclaimed a woman, and he knew at once that he was wrong; this was Gwendoline, not one of the Armitage sisters. He frowned as Gwendoline rushed on, as if she had quite forgotten that she had snubbed and evaded him. 'Oh, Rolly, can you come here at once?'

'Where?' asked Rollison.

'To the house—our house, Barrington House,' said Gwendoline and then she broke off and another voice spoke but Rollison could not catch the words.   'Oh, all right,' said Gwendoline, in an aside, and added: 'Rolly, mother wants a word with you.'

'Oh, Rolly,' said Hilda, after a moment's pause.   She was more breathless than her daughter and he could tell that she was in a state of great agitation, 'please *do* come over, David has disappeared.'

'Disappeared?' echoed Rollison, sharply.

'Yes, into thin air,' said Hilda.   'I'm so terribly worried, please do come.'

CHAPTER TEN

Insult For The Lady

IT WAS ON the tip of Rollison's tongue to say that he could not leave the flat and to ask them to visit him but he changed his mind and said:

'I can't come for half an hour, Hilda. Have you told the police.'

'No,' said Hilda. 'No, of course not. I mean—no, well I don't want to until I've seen you; Rolly, do come earlier if you can.'

'I may bring a friend,' said Rollison.

'Bring anyone you like,' said Hilda, distractedly, 'but do come.'

'I'll come,' promised Rollison. 'Stay there and don't get worked up.' He rang off and stood looking at the telephone, conscious of a deep disappointment because the *tête-à-tête* seemed over for that night. Then he telephoned Anstey and found that Jolly was there. He told Jolly to take everything to Barrington House, then had a word with the old solicitor; were there any rumours about Barrington-Ley in the City?

'There are vague hints and suggestions,' said Anstey. 'They don't add up to much but they're not very reassuring. It would be better if he were in London instead of in the country. I even heard of a rumour that he has left the country but I can't believe that of Barrington-Ley. In any case, he has been seen in the City during the last week. I hope you've discovered nothing against him.'

'Nothing,' said Rollison, 'but I know that his family is worried about his health.'

'Health,' echoed Anstey, sceptically.

'Health,' repeated Rollison, firmly, 'and don't go reading more into that than I mean.' He learned that Anstey was able to supply all the gramophone records that he wanted and rang off. Grice had not renewed his suggestion that there was something wrong with Barrington-Ley's affairs but if the rumours now worried Anstey, Grice would know all about them.

He telephoned Scotland Yard again; Grice was still there.

'Give me a chance,' he protested when he heard Rollison's voice, 'I've sent for your maid but she's off duty and won't be here for half an hour. I'll brief her myself.'

'Send her to Barrington House, will you,' said Rollison. 'She's to say that I hired her for Lady Lost.'

'Why Barrington House?' demanded Grice.

'Because they have a very fine radiogram,' said Rollison, cryptically. 'Good-bye, old chap.'

He was smiling when he rang off—and then his smile changed to one of anticipation for he saw the spare bedroom door open.

For the second time he watched the Lady of Lost Memory walking towards him.

She was transformed!

Her hair, no longer braided, was dressed Victorian fashion and looked not brown but burnished copper. Two combs with jewelled backs glinted beneath the light. Her cheeks had a glow, make-up actually improving on nature; her eyes glowed, too; and her lips were enticing.

At her breast was a single *diamanté* star, a paste copy of a famous jewel which had come Rollison's way when he had been involved in a case where jewel-thieves had turned their hands to murder, and on her fingers two rings, also of paste but, at a quick glance, indistinguishable from the real thing. Nearly as tall as Rollison, not slim but with a figure to make most men's heartbeats quicken, she stood in front of him.

'*Superb!*' said Rollison.

'You like it?'

'Like it is not the word. I marvel at it. Who taught you to walk, Lady Lost?'

'Lady Lost?' She looked startled.

'That is a figure of speech,' said Rollison. 'How do you feel?'

'Happier than I can remember!'

'Splendid!' He stood back, still looking at her, and added with a twinge of reluctance: 'We're going out for an hour or two, to some friends of yours– the Barrington-Leys.'

She also looked regretful.

'They have been so kind to me, but—'

'I think it's wise to go,' Rollison said, gently, 'we might get your memory back.'

She said, very slowly:

'I have been thinking as I looked into the mirror,' she said. 'I have not remembered and yet, somewhere within me, there is a feeling that I shall not like it when I know who I am; it is as if some horrid thing happened, something which made me forget things which I always wanted to forget.' She held out her hand. 'Please understand me.'

'I think I understand,' said Rollison. 'You may be right but behind that, further back in the years, there will be good things, well worth remembering.'

'Can you be sure?'

Rollison smiled. 'You didn't become what you are to-night by accident. This is the real you!'

While they were waiting for a taxi he helped her on with her coat, wondering whether Grice had sent her dress and the coat to every dressmaker of consequence in London. Molyneaux might not have made the gown but could well know whence it had come.

He went out without a coat and found it surprisingly cold—her mink was not superfluous. As they waited by the kerb he looked about him but saw no shadowy figures suggesting that they were being watched.

The lost lady said:

'You have asked few questions, Mr Rollison.'

'Very few,' he said.

'Do you not even want to know where I went from the nursing home?'

It was much better for her to volunteer information than for him to ask for it and he was sorry that the belated taxi chose that moment to arrive. He gave the address and then sat back in the taxi.

'A man was waiting for me,' she said, suddenly.

'Where?'

'At the corner of the street.'

'A young man or an old one?'

'A young man—younger, yes, younger than you. A good-looking man, who was very amiable. He first took me to a café and we had tea. He said very little, only that you were most anxious to see me. We went then to a small house, I do not know where. I rested there while he was out. Then, when he returned, he put me into a taxi and gave the driver your address. That is *all*.'

'Had you ever seen him before?'

'Never. He said that he was a friend of yours.'

'I see,' said Rollison.

He did not see for the incident of the young man simply made more mystery.

The taxi pulled up outside Barrington House and as they climbed out the door opened and the footman appeared. He bowed as the woman passed him and inclined his head to Rollison. In his manner there remained a faint suggestion of insolence.

'Madam is waiting for you, sir,' he said.

Rollison manoeuvred so that he could see into the big drawing-room as his companion entered. She walked as if she were used to such houses and such company. He could not see her face but he saw Hilda's and Gwendoline's. He hoped to see something more than surprise—and he did so but only a hint of mortification and displeasure on Gwendoline's.

Hilda recovered from her surprise and held out both hands.

'My dear, how wonderful to see you well again.'

'You are very kind,' said Lady Lost.

'Gwen, isn't it wonderful?' cried Hilda.

Gwendoline said that it was and smiled distantly. Although it was evening, she was dressed in light-coloured tweeds, her hair was untidy and she looked tired and restless. Hilda was in a dark green cocktail dress. The three women presented a remarkable contrast. Gwendoline, as if fresh from the country, sturdy, lacking all the qualities of allurement which were so lavished on Lady Lost and Hilda, *petite* and almost bird-like.

'You have come to stay with us, I hope,' said Hilda. 'Yes, you must, I will not take no for an answer. Gwendoline will show you your room, you will want to take off your coat.'

Lady Lost hesitated.

'Yes,' said Rollison. 'Of course.'

'Gwen!' called Hilda, with a note of command. Reluctantly Gwendoline came forward, as reluctantly the other woman went with her. When the door closed Hilda stopped pretending and through the social mask Rollison saw the anxiety and the fear that lurked within her. 'Rolly,' she said, 'did you *have* to bring her now?'

'Yes,' said Rollison.

'How can we talk in front of her? I sent Gwen out with her but they will not stay for long, there is no time—'

'We can make the best of what there is,' said Rollison. 'What's this about David?'

She said: 'He has *completely* disappeared.'

'Since when?'

'Two days ago. He left Sussex and said that he would return the same evening and, when he did not arrive, I telephoned his office where his secretary was still working—Rolly, he had left to catch the train! I telephoned here and he had not been seen. I thought perhaps the train was delayed but no, it was on time. I waited for the next train and the next, and—' She broke off and looked suddenly broken, as if something had been taken away from her. 'He's just—gone, Rolly.'

'What did you do about it yesterday?' asked Rollison.

'Nothing. I—we—kept hoping.'

The door opened abruptly and Gwendoline strode in, closing it behind her. She was tight-lipped and angry.

'You might have had the decency to warn us if you couldn't leave her behind.'

'Gwen!' reproved Hilda.

'Well, couldn't he?' demanded Gwen. 'But there isn't time for recriminations, she'll be down in five minutes if I know anything about her, she won't want to miss a word! Have you told Rolly about father?'

'Yes, of course,' said Hilda.

Rollison stepped to the fireplace and stood with his back towards it, paying more attention to Gwendoline.

'Will you help us to find David?' she demanded.

'Yes,' said Rollison. 'If you will tell me the whole truth.'

'But Rolly—' began Hilda and then her voice trailed off.

'Why did you do nothing yesterday?' demanded Rollison. 'You were worried the night before last, you say, but you didn't tell me and you don't appear to have told the police.'

Hilda said: 'We kept hoping against hope, because we don't want a scandal. We must give David every chance to—to—' Her voice trailed off again.

'To do what?' demanded Rollison.

'To give the lie to those damned hypocrites who are spreading the story that he is in difficulties,' said Gwendoline, in a low-pitched voice. 'He isn't, he can't be! And I tell you that this woman whom you thought fit to bring along here to-night is responsible. Oh, I can see that she had duped you; I suppose that isn't difficult if you're foreign and a little unusual but she has no more lost her memory than I have!'

She broke off and coloured furiously for the door had opened and the Lady Lost stood there, so exquisitely gowned and so lovely, with the smile frozen on her lips and a hopeless expression in her eyes.

'Mr Rollison,' she said, quietly, 'please take me away from here.'

'My dear!' cried Hilda, 'you are warmly welcome; my daughter is distraught or she would not have said such a thing.' She looked distractedly at Gwen. 'Gwen, please, apologise for the hateful thing you said.'

Gwen looked steadily at the woman in the doorway, and spoke in a low-pitched voice, hardly moving her lips.

'Her memory is as good as yours and mine,' she said.

'Gwen!'

'Ask her to deny it,' sneered Gwendoline.

The woman in the doorway turned slowly and walked into the hall, carrying herself proudly and yet giving an impression that she had become deeply despondent and hurt. Hilda hurried after her. Gwendoline took a cigarette from a box on the table, lit it and returned Rollison's steady gaze.

'Do you really believe that?' he demanded.

'Yes, and so will you, unless you're completely under her domination.'

Rollison said: 'I see. And under whose influence did you refuse to tell me or the police about David, until to-night, and why are you still anxious not to let the police know that he has disappeared?'

She backed away, the colour now going from her face.

'Answer me,' said Rollison, roughly. 'Who persuaded you to let him be away for two days?' When she did not answer, he went on with a hard note in his voice: 'You've damned his reputation. Until he's found, *if* he's found, there will be a panic in the City, everything in which he has an interest will go to pieces. If you had wanted to ruin him you couldn't have chosen a better way.' When she still remained silent, he added bitterly: 'But perhaps you do want to ruin him.'

'Rolly!'

'You're behaving as if you do,' said Rollison.

Hilda was still talking outside and intermingled with her words was the voice of a man. It was Jolly. Jolly would not let Lady Lost go unaccompanied. Rollison stood looking at Gwendoline.

'Well, who was it?' he demanded.

In a low voice, she said: 'Pomeroy.'

'The little fat man?'

'Yes.'

'The firm of Pomeroy, Ward & Pomeroy deny all knowledge of him,' said Rollison. 'Who told you that the man's name was Pomeroy and what gave him the authority to make you keep silent about David for so long?'

She said: 'David—brought him here. He seemed to trust him. He—Pomeroy—telephoned us yesterday. David should have kept an appointment with him yesterday evening but did not. Pomeroy advised us to say nothing; he felt sure that David would come back before long.'

'You trust Pomeroy and yet distrust the woman?' Then, when he saw the hurt in her eyes, Rollison relented and rested a hand on her shoulder. 'Don't worry too much, Gwen. We'll find him—but we must know everything and the police must be told at once.'

'That's—impossible.'

'You've a wrong idea of the police, too,' said Rollison. 'Is there anything else?'

'The rumours,' said Gwen.

'They didn't start by accident,' said Rollison.

He left her and hurried to the hall. Jolly was standing by a table on which was a pile of gramophone records in cardboard containers, as well as a coffee-pot, looking incongruous against the panelled background of the hall. Dressed again in her furs, Lady Lost was standing by Hilda's side and Hilda was saying:

'Of course I understand. I am so very sorry. Please do forgive my daughter.'

'Jolly,' said Rollison, going to his side, 'have you a taxi waiting?'
'Yes, sir.'

'Then take the records, the coffee and Lady Lost back to the flat,' said Rollison. 'I'll get there as soon as I can.'

'Very good, sir,' said Jolly.

The Lady of Lost Memory looked at Rollison and smiled, a shadow of the smile he had seen at the flat. The footman was standing impassively by the door. Jolly picked up the records, which were heavy for him to carry in one load.

'Help him, please.'

'Very good, sir,' said the footman and Jolly, relieved of half the records, took the coffee-pot from the table and walked sedately to the porch.

Rollison watched them get into the taxi and looked up and down, still afraid of some unknown thing to which he could not put a name. Slowly and reluctantly he turned back to the house. The footman walked a pace behind him

Both exclaimed aloud!

From the shadows of the garden a man appeared, a short, thin man who was clearly visible against the light from the hall as he ran up the steps and into the house, then darted out of sight. Hilda screamed. Rollison sprinted. He saw the man turn into the drawing-room, heard an exclamation from Gwendoline—and then he reached the room and saw the knife which was hurtling through the air towards the girl. She stood as if petrified. Rollison shouted:

'Move, Gwen!'

He flung himself forward but he knew that he would be too late. The knife seemed to miss Gwendoline but, before he reached her, he saw blood welling from a cut in her neck. The little man who had thrown the knife turned and made for the door, like a rat at bay. He thought that Rollison was concerned only for Gwen and did not notice him swing round and put out his foot. The man ran into it and pitched headlong. He fell by the feet of Hilda, in the doorway. Then she rushed towards Gwendoline.

She impeded Rollison who tried to dodge round her but she went the same way. He saw the little man pick himself up and rush into the hall. The footman was standing like a man struck dumb. He made no effort to stop the attacker and when Rollison reached the hall the front door slammed.

Rollison glared at the footman who still stood petrified.

'What is your name?'

'Farrow, sir.'

'Telephone for a doctor at once, Farrow.'

'Er—yes, sir. A doctor, yes, sir. Who—'

'The family doctor, Dr Renfrew,' said Rollison and he turned and went back into the room. There Hilda was bending over Gwendoline who was sitting, ashen-faced, in an upright chair. Blood was welling freely from the wound in her neck but the cut was not deep enough to cause serious harm. He padded a handkerchief while Hilda dabbed ineffectually with a tiny piece of lace. He pressed the pad against the cut, which was two inches long, then lifted her so that her neck pressed against his shoulder, keeping the pad in position.

'Will you lead the way?' he said to Hilda.

The walk seemed interminable but at last they turned into a large, high-ceilinged bedroom, furnished with maple with a furry, thick-piled carpet and a silk-draped bed. Hilda turned down the bedclothes and Rollison, managing to keep the pad in position so as to stop the bleeding, laid the girl down.

'A doctor!' exclaimed Hilda. 'We must have Andrew!'

'I've sent for him,' said Rollison: 'Don't worry, it's not serious.'

'Not—serious,' echoed Hilda and from her too-bright eyes Rollison thought that she would faint. 'She might—'

'I—am—all right,' Gwendoline said. The words were an effort. Rollison wished she had not spoken for the muscles of her neck moved and another crimson stain appeared on the edge of the handkerchief.

'Don't talk, Gwen,' he said. 'Hilda, hold the pad in position. He let Hilda take over and then asked: 'Where will we find cotton wool?'

Before she answered a maid appeared, carrying a first-aid box— the first practical thing done at the house that night. Rollison gave her an appreciative smile, opened the box and took out cotton wool, making it into a pad to replace the handkerchief. He applied the new dressing while the maid went out to get some hot water. He stood by the bed, looking towards the door—and as he stared, a man appeared, a little fat man now dressed in a dinner jacket suit but unmistakably the man whom 'David called Pomeroy'.

CHAPTER ELEVEN

Coffee And Records

THE MAN STARED blankly at Rollison, as if he had never seen him before. Rollison could not move from the bedside. Hilda turned and backed a pace.

'What has happened?' asked the little fat man.

He had a gentle deceptive voice, with no heartiness, and there was now nothing about him to give the impression that he was a sporting gent. He smiled soberly at Hilda and stood looking down at Gwendoline. He did not seem shocked at the sight of blood.

'What has happened?' he repeated. 'Who are you, sir?'

Rollison said: 'How is your nose?'

'*Nose*?' asked the fat man, startled.

'You appear to have a bad memory,' said Rollison.

It was an impossible situation and he was infuriated by his help-lessness but he did not trust Hilda to maintain the right pressure and he had to stay where he was. There was no glint in the fat man's eyes, only bewilderment. Even Gwendoline would believe the two men had never met before.

Then came hurried footsteps and a youngish man entered the room carrying a small attaché case. He was tall and well-dressed and had anxiety written clearly upon his countenance. This was Dr Renfrew, good-looking and surprisingly young and 'Andrew' to Hilda Barrington-Ley. Renfrew recovered himself quickly and advanced to the bed.

The maid came in with a bowl of hot water and towels.

Rollison said: 'It's a knife wound in the neck.'

'Knife!' exclaimed Renfrew. He bent over the patient. The maid stood by. A middle-aged woman who could be relied on to keep her head. The fat man stood near the door, watching the proceedings with a puzzled stare.

Rollison said to Hilda: 'We'll wait downstairs.'

He put a hand on the fat man's arm and led the way out of the room. The other did not protest and they went down side by side. Their footsteps were muffled by the thick carpet. Rollison led the way into the drawing-room, where a few spots of blood were congealing on the cream carpet, and closed the door.

Puzzled eyes, but eyes which Rollison was not likely to forget, contemplated him.

'You bewilder me, sir,' said the fat man. 'Who are you?'

'My name is Rollison,' said Rollison, heavily. He went across the room, picked up the knife by the blade and put it on the piano. 'And we have met before.'

'Not to my recollection,' said the fat man.

'At the office of Pomeroy, Ward & Pomeroy,' said Rollison, wondering whether there was any way in which he could make the man admit the truth.

The reaction to his words was curious. The other widened his small eyes to their fullest, opened his lips to a round 'O' and raised his podgy hands with the fingers outstretched, rather as if he had suffered an electric shock. He stood looking at Rollison until Rollison's annoyance faded and he laughed.

'That infamous den!' exclaimed the fat man, in a voice squeaky with indignation. 'I am insulted!' I have not set foot in that place for years *and* I never shall again. I have parted company with *all* the people connected with the firm and—'

He broke off, narrowed his eyes, closed his mouth and let his arms fall. 'Sir,' he said, with dignity, 'I demand an explanation.'

'You may keep on demanding,' said Rollison.

'I trust you are now convinced that you are mistaken.'

'I am not convinced one little bit,' said Rollison. 'Did you know that Marcus Shayle was under arrest?'

Into the little eyes there sprang a wary glint. It took the man several moments to recover enough to ask who Marcus Shayle was. Rollison gave up trying. He had to, in any case, for the woman detective arrived from Grice. He made sure she knew exactly what to say to Lady Lost and sent her to Gresham Terrace. The 'maid' was a meek-looking, mild-mannered but powerful woman and Rollison had no doubt that in a struggle she would be able to give a good account of herself. She would watch the Lady of Lost Memory with eagle eye.

Rollison was on edge to return to the flat but there were other things to do. He went out by the side door, unobserved, and telephoned

Scotland Yard. Late though it was, Grice was still there. Rollison told him exactly what had happened, including the reluctance of the Barrington-Leys to inform the police and he made a special point of mentioning the little fat man.

'Are you formally asking me to come over?' Grice asked.

'No,' said Rollison, 'but I'll persuade Hilda Barrington-Ley to send for you—be patient for an hour or so, will you? There's nothing that can usefully be done yet.'

'Did you see this man with the knife clearly?'

Rollison gave a description as best he could, then rang off and walked back to the house. No one appeared to have missed him. Pomeroy was still in the drawing-room and he tried to freeze Rollison with a glance. Then Hilda came into the room with the young doctor.

She now introduced Dr Renfrew, whom she continued to call Andrew. Rollison liked the look of the man, who smiled faintly as Hilda talked about the shock the attack had given her and how fortunate it was that Rollison had acted so promptly. Renfrew interrupted her when she paused for breath, looking at Rollison as if for support.

'Mrs Barrington-Ley is reluctant to go to the police and I have told her that she must do so.'

'You'll have to report it, won't you?' said Rollison.

'Yes,' said Renfrew, promptly. 'I don't want to act against your wishes, Mrs Barrington-Ley, but —'

'Andrew, if we hadn't told you how it happened you would never have known. If it were suicide, you wouldn't talk such nonsense.'

'That would be a different matter,' said Renfrew.

Rollison said: 'Hilda, my sweet, Gwendoline was within a few inches of losing her life.' He picked the knife up from the piano and Hilda gasped. 'Dr Renfrew knows he must tell the police. If you persuade him not to, it will only make things awkward for him, because I am going to see the police very soon.'

'Rolly!'

'And,' continued Rollison, 'I am going to tell them that David is missing.'

'You are not!' cried Pomeroy.

It was the first time he had taken part in the conversation, and he made Renfrew start. The doctor's dark, sleek hair and rather aquiline face gave him quite a presence but the way he looked then made him seem very young. He was nearly as tall as Rollison and he dwarfed Pomeroy, who came strutting forward and put a hand on Hilda's arm.

'Aren't we?' murmured Rollison.

'If you consider it your duty to inform the police of this dastardly attack on Gwendoline, then I am in full agreement,' said Pomeroy, 'but to acquaint them of the fact that David is missing will be to heap coals upon the fire of rumour now sweeping through the City. Such an action would be a betrayal of friendship, would perhaps do incalculable harm to a great and good man. I have no doubt that there are excellent reasons for David's protracted absence and I insist that no such report is made to the police.'

He eyed Rollison, not with anger but with indignation, and his grip on Hilda's arm tightened. It was easy to see how simple it had been for him to influence the others earlier.

'Mr Pomeroy, I do not like your advice,' Rollison said mildly.

'Like it or not as you wish, sir, but it is advice which takes into consideration the reputation of a very fine character and, if that were not enough, it affects the happiness and the domestic joy of a woman whom I admire and esteem so much that I will exert myself in every way, to the very limit of my endurance, to prevent you from committing this cardinal tactical error. I do not know you, sir. I believe that we have some cause to be grateful for your prompt action when Gwendoline was injured but I do not see that as justification for such an attitude as you are now adopting. Have you no loyalty towards Hilda?'

'So much that I am advising her for her own good.' He looked at Renfrew. 'What do you think?'

'I had no idea that Mr Barrington-Ley was missing,' said Renfrew, worriedly, 'but if no one knows where he is, then it would be wise to tell the police.'

'That is intolerable presumption, Doctor,' said Pomeroy coldly. 'I for*bid* this story to be placed before the police, to allow it to be handed out to the Press, that it may be blazoned across the headlines of the daily newspapers in the morning, to let it create a panic selling on the Stock Exchange, to undermine the good name and the security of the many companies in which my dear friend David has an interest. Understand, sir—I forbid it!'

Rollison let him finish then stepped towards Hilda, removed Pomeroy's hand, drew Hilda towards him and said:

'Hilda, they tried to kill Gwendoline. They have probably kidnapped David. He is, at this moment, in acute danger. I can't help to save him unless the police know. Do you understand me—David is in *acute* danger.'

'I declare—' began Pomeroy.

'Be quiet!' snapped Rollison.

The man opened his mouth and closed it again and then backed away. Hilda stared, aghast, into Rollison's eyes and then went slowly across the room towards the telephone. She picked up the receiver.

'What is the number?' she asked.

'Whitehall 1212,' said Rollison.

He watched Pomeroy closely. The man was angry and disappointed and Rollison thought that he was afraid but he preserved a dignified silence. Rollison went to Hilda's side, told her to ask for Grice and, when she had spoken to the Superintendent, gave him a summary of what had happened, to make sure that Hilda and the others knew that it would be useless to go back on their word. He rang off and said:

'The police will be here within twenty minutes. Sit down and rest, Hilda. Gwendoline is all right, isn't she?'

'She will be,' said Renfrew. 'It isn't serious.

'Good!' said Rollison, leading Hilda to a chair. 'Can you stay here until the police arrive, Renfrew?'

'I intend to do so,' said Renfrew.

'Then I needn't stay,' said Rollison. 'Will you see that the knife is left, untouched, on the piano?'

He went out, opening the front door himself. The footman who had shown such veiled insolence, and who had affected to be stupefied instead of stopping the little man with the knife, was nowhere to be seen. As Rollison sauntered along the road, the chimes of a nearby clock struck midnight. He frowned at the lateness of the hour but he did not go far, walking back towards Barrington House on the opposite side of the road. There was a street lamp near the front gate and he expected to see Pomeroy come out.

When Grice arrived, the clock was striking the quarter, Rollison walked away; Pomeroy had either used a side entrance or was still inside the house.

Jolly was standing by the radiogram in a corner of the big room at the flat and Lady Lost was leaning back in an easy chair with her eyes closed and a faint smile at her lips. Rollison entered the room and Jolly bowed slightly and motioned to the radiogram. Rollison nodded. When the last record was played, a bright and lively waltz by Johann Strauss, Jolly stopped the disc and inquired:

'Is there anything you require, sir?'

'Let's have some coffee,' said Rollison.

'Very good, sir.' Jolly went out and Rollison stood looking at Lady Lost. She had opened her eyes and was looking at him. The smile had died and something of the hurt she had suffered at Barrington House showed on her face; it was as if she were keeping her eyes half-closed to prevent him from seeing the hurt in them.

He could not understand the turmoil in his mind.

This woman might be a fraud; Gwendoline might be right; but he desired above all else to prove that Lady Lost was innocent of all chicanery; he wanted to believe her memory gone and longed to restore it.

At last she broke the silence.

'Please do not talk of what happened. It is—forgotten.'

'Is it?' asked Rollison, slowly.

'Yes, and it does not matter. The girl dislikes me. Once she came to see me at the hospital and then it was clear—she dislikes and distrusts me and who can be blamed for talking as she did of a person whom one does not trust?'

'There's something in that,' said Rollison. He offered cigarettes but she refused. He lit one, slowly. 'She says that you know her father and that you saw him several times before you appeared at Barrington House.'

The woman sat up, her eyes ablaze.

'Then where is he? *Where is he?* If he saw me then he can name me!'

'He has gone away,' said Rollison, gently.

'To where? How long must I wait?'

'No one knows where,' said Rollison.

She looked acutely disappointed; he could not bring himself to believe it was feigned. She stared at him with her eyes wide open and her lips parted.

'Has he—been hurt?' she asked.

'I don't know,' said Rollison.

'You would tell me if that were so,' she said.

'Yes. Listen to me. *Bar-ring-ton-Ley.*' He uttered each syllable carefully. 'Had you heard it *before* you went to their home?'

'I do not know,' she said. 'I just do not know.'

He smiled.

'I shouldn't have worried you with that, just now.' Jolly came in with the coffee and some biscuits. 'Pour out, Jolly, please,' said Rollison and stepped towards the radiogram. Four records were spread out on top—the National Anthems of Yugoslavia, Greece, Rumania and Bulgaria. The coffee in that tiny pot was of a kind popular in the Balkans and the Middle East.

'Please, I do not like coffee,' said the lady.

'Try this,' said Rollison, 'just to please me.'

At the first sip, her expression altered; she looked almost startled and she stared at the cup, then at Rollison, while Jolly stood hopefully by the door and Rollison, without turning his head, put the needle in position and switched on the radiogram. The first strains of the Yugoslav National Anthem came softly from the record while the visitor sipped the coffee again and said:

'This is remarkable! It is—'

She stopped abruptly.

The tune was clearer now, after the opening bars. Played in slow time by a massed band, the volume swelled and filled the room—but Rollison was not listening. He was oblivious of everything but Lady Lost who was leaning forward in her chair, her eyes shining, the cup and saucer trembling in her hand. She did not speak but she put the coffee down and rose slowly to her feet, moving towards him as if in a dream.

She reached his side and they stood together while the music came like a magic which had touched some hidden chord and brought to her eyes ineffable delight.

CHAPTER TWELVE

Memory At Bay

THE ANTHEM ENDED...

The Lady of Lost Memory stood looking at Rollison. Rollison switched off and silence fell.

The radiance in her eyes lasted for a long time and then began to fade, so slowly that at first he thought it was a trick of the light. He had never wanted anything more deeply than to hear her say that she could remember.

The radiance became a glow and in her eyes there was a tinge of anxiety. The smile also faded and abruptly she turned away.

She said: 'That is my National Anthem, I am a Serb. I can recall incidents of my childhood, little, inconsequential incidents; they came to me as I stood there and I have them with me now—but that is all.'

'It's a beginning,' said Rollison, forcing himself to be brisk. He looked at the records and sorted several out then motioned to Jolly to attend to the radiogram while he stepped out to the woman's side, smiling as if they had cause to congratulate each other. 'And a good beginning,' he said. 'Sit down and listen for a while.'

He had selected Serbian tunes. They followed one upon another, bringing into the flat an atmosphere of rugged land and gypsy music, the plucking of strings and the thin tone of flutes, all with a quality of its own whether gay or sad.

All the time Rollison watched her but she was sitting with her eyes closed and her face quite expressionless. When all were finished, Rollison waited hopefully. Jolly began to pack up the records but he also was watching Lady Lost. She looked as if she had fallen asleep but when Rollison stirred she opened her eyes, smiled, and said:

'I am very tired.'

'And you must get to bed!' said Rollison, promptly. 'The maid will get you anything you want.'

'Whatever I remember,' said the lady, 'I shall not forget you, Mr Rollison! Good-night.' She held out her hand and Rollison pressed it, then she turned away towards the spare room and Jolly stood waiting.

'No Watson to my Holmes to-night,' said Rollison, 'Holmes was never as empty-headed as I am now.'

'You are tired, sir,' murmured Jolly. 'You have succeeded in touching familiar chords, sir, which no one else contrived.'

Rollison smiled. 'They didn't have the opportunity,' he said. 'There are limits to what one can do in a nursing home.'

'I question very much whether the people at the nursing home did all they could to help to restore madame's memory.'

'They were under medical supervision,' Rollison reminded him.

'You will remember, sir,' said Jolly, 'that Dr Renfrew is the family physician of the Barrington-Leys.'

'And Dr Cray is a hard-bitten police surgeon,' said Rollison.

'Of course, sir. We do not know, however, what instructions Dr Cray gave to the matron and we don't know whether they were carried out. You will forgive me for saying so, sir, but anyone who wished to revive a lost memory might attempt to do so with music—it is, I believe, an elementary process in the practice of a psychologist. Why has it not been tried?'

'She's been ill,' Rollison said. Out of talks with Jolly much that was obscure often came to light.

'Our inquiries at the nursing home elicited the information that Lady Lost was still suffering from the effects of the poison,' said Jolly, 'but she came straight from there to here and we cannot say that she is in poor health at the moment. Obviously she made an excellent recovery but we were not given that impression when we last inquired, four days ago.'

'No, we weren't,' agreed Rollison.

'If we were to find out what instructions Dr Cray gave, we could then find out from the lady whether they were carried out,' said Jolly.

'It'll be my first job in the morning,' said Rollison.

'I am glad that the suggestion finds favour, sir,' said Jolly.

'There are one or two other matters of which you have doubtless thought. If we were to take the coat and the dress to a furrier and dressmaker, we might learn more.'

'I had made a note of that one,' said Rollison, 'but Grice has probably tried it.'

'I doubt it, sir. There were no name tags or maker's tags and I think it likely that the police will have been satisfied with that, especially since the lingerie was of American manufacture. That is another interesting point, sir; I think we might make inquiries in America. A photograph would reach there in a very short time if sent by air and your friends in New York would undoubtedly be only too glad to help.'

'You're getting better, better and better,' said Rollison.

'Thank you,' murmured Jolly. 'Then there is yet another matter, one which you can hardly be expected to have discovered, sir. In the last few weeks I have taken the liberty of making certain inquiries and, while none of them appear to have any great importance, there is a factor which I am sure will interest you. I made the acquaintance of the butler at Barrington House and several others of the staff. Two things emerged, sir. First, that Farrow the footman whom we saw tonight was engaged only recently with the approval of the plump Mr Pomeroy.'

'Was he, by George!'

'He was, sir, and the staff dislike him very much indeed,' said Jolly. 'In fact they have the impression that Farrow was engaged by Mrs Barrington-Ley *because* Mr Pomeroy—requested it.'

'Or ordered it,' said Rollison.

Jolly smiled. 'The butler has a very neat turn of phrase, sir. The subject of the footman was not discussed until last evening. The other matter I have known for some time but I did not at that juncture see what useful purpose would be served by advising you.'

'Out with it,' urged Rollison.

'The butler believes that Dr Renfrew has an understanding with Miss Gwendoline. In fact he is a friend of the family which doubtless explains why so youthful a doctor is employed. I have tried to get details as to Dr Renfrew's reputation and I must say that in the profession he has the reputation of being a brilliant young doctor and he is very well-liked by the staff at Barrington House.'

'I see,' said Rollison, a trifle heavily. 'I'll have a shot at Renfrew, too. Farrow seemed reluctant to send for him I remember—that's worth keeping in mind.' He stifled a yawn. 'I think we'll get to bed. Where have you put the maid?'

'In my room, sir,' said Jolly, getting up at once.

'And what about you?'

'I shall put two chairs together in the hall and be perfectly comfortable, I assure you.'

'I see,' said Rollison. 'You're a good chap, Jolly.' He was getting into bed when the telephone rang. He had an extension on a bedside table and settled himself on the pillows before he answered. He saw Jolly's shadow near the door.

'Hallo,' he said.

'Rolly,' said Grice, and Rollison sat up. 'I'm sorry it's so late,' went on Grice, 'but there are one or two things I must know now.'

'Fire away,' said Rollison.

'What do you make of the footman at Barrington House?'

'Precious little, except that I wouldn't trust him an inch,' said Rollison. 'He could have caught the little man with the knife.'

'I see,' said Grice. 'It doesn't much matter about that—*we've* caught the little man.'

'*What?*' exclaimed Rollison and Grice laughed in triumph.

'I thought that would shake you. There was a man answering your description whom we knew lived in London and who has been known to use a knife, so we pulled him in and he talked.'

'This is progress!' exclaimed Rollison. 'Has he talked much?'

'He says that he was hired to kill Gwendoline Barrington-Ley but he can't or won't give us the name or description of the man who hired him. The order seems to have passed through several channels. You know how these things work.'

'East End channels?' demanded Rollison.

'Yes.'

'Well, well,' said Rollison, 'I'll slip down there in the morning— that's what you want me to do, isn't it?'

'It might be helpful,' said Grice. 'As for the footman—one of my men thinks he has seen him before. We've got his prints and they're not in the records, so he hasn't passed through our hands. You haven't seen him before, have you?'

'No,' said Rollison.

'We'll have to do what we can,' said Grice and broke off, making a curious noise into the telephone. 'Sorry,' he apologised, 'that was a yawn. Have you learned anything from the lady?'

'She is a Serb,' said Rollison. 'I thought she was going to regain her memory to-night but it faded out again.'

'H'm, yes,' said Grice sceptically.

'Now what's the matter?' demanded Rollison, sharply.

'Has she ever lost it?' asked Grice.

'What makes you think she might be foxing?' demanded Rollison, stretching his hand out for his cigarette case. As he fumbled with it, Jolly came into the room, took out a cigarette, lit it in a holder and handed it to Rollison.

'Cray doubts very much whether her mind's as blank as she says it is,' said Grice. 'He told the matron to try her out with music and we had a shot at Yugoslav national music as well as other from the Balkans. Reaction, nil. There isn't much doubt that you're right and she's a Serb—I had an expert have a look at her, quite early, and he said Serb or anyway Slav without any doubt. There are also other indications.'

'Oh,' said Rollison. 'What about Renfrew's opinion?'

Grice chuckled again.

'He's a very bright young man, most impressionable, and rather like you—if a handsome woman says she's lost her memory he's too much of a gentleman to doubt it.'

'I see,' said Rollison, heavily. 'One for and one against. Did it ever occur to you to make sure that the test was carried out?'

'Now, come,' said Grice, 'that's a reputable nursing home and, in this case, the matron would obviously be so eager to make up for the slip that was made.'

'You're more trusting than I am,' said Rollison, 'but then, you're a policeman!'

Grice laughed.

'As a matter of fact, Rolly, I'm very pleased with the day's work. We've Shayle, as you know, and this little man with the knife. Also— we know one name under which your lost lady is known.'

Rollison shot a glance at Jolly, and said:

'More guesswork?'

'No,' said Grice. 'We had her clothes examined. The dress didn't help us much but a leading London furrier said that he was sure that the coat came from Loudens, of New York. Loudens have a kind of trade mark in their work, one which only a few people know. So we radioed a photograph to Loudens and another to the New York police—what's that?'

'I groaned,' said Rollison, glumly. 'All right, she bought the coat in New York. What's her name?'

'Lila Hollern,' said Grice. 'At least, she called herself the Countess Hollern and signed her cheques Lila. She was in America for six months, raising money—she said—for the Yugoslav earthquake Relief Fund.'

Rollison interrupted: 'Countess Hollern isn't a Serbian name.'

'She said she was married to an Austrian count,' said Grice, 'and that her husband was a political prisoner for some years. He is now supposed to be in Belgrade. Everyone in New York thought her wonderful, she raised nearly half a million dollars—and disappeared with it!'

'Are these facts?' demanded Rollison, sharply.

'The money was in her name at the New York bank,' said Grice, 'and was transferred to an account in England a month ago. We haven't yet tackled the English bank; they're touchy on inquiries, you know, and I doubt whether I shall be able to get a Court Order for an examination of her account just yet—but I hope to, soon.'

'What about the Relief Fund?' asked Rollison, with sinking heart.

'The London people only knew about her from New York,' said Grice, who was remarkably cheerful, 'and she certainly convinced them in New York. I shall have a full report by cable soon. The money disappeared, there's no doubt about that.'

'So did the Countess,' murmured Rollison.

Grice said gently:

'I hate to disillusion you, Rolly, but she did turn up in remarkable circumstances at Mrs B-L's first big effort for a Relief Fund, didn't she? Had she not been poisoned, she might by now have been an active member of that fund, raking in more money.'

'Oh, yes,' said Rollison, 'but it might not have been quite so simple. If you can stand an awkward question—why was she poisoned?'

'Do you have to ask?' demanded Grice. 'Obviously because she is one of several people involved in the swindle. The other members did not like to think that she was to be questioned by the police. They much preferred to see her dead. That is a strong enough motive even for you.'

'It's very ingenious,' murmured Rollison.

'I don't think there's much the matter with it,' said Grice, complacently. 'Nor will you, when you know that Messrs Pomeroy, Ward & Pomeroy are handling the accounts of the London Branch of the Relief Fund, as well as Barrington-Ley's accounts. It all ties up very nicely, doesn't it?'

CHAPTER THIRTEEN

East End

ROLLISON AGREED THAT it did appear to tie up very nicely, said good-bye, replaced the receiver and stared blankly into Jolly's face. After a while he gave the gist of the conversation, whereupon Jolly's hopefulness faded and was replaced by his habitual expression of gloom.

'The only bright spot,' said Rollison, 'is that he doesn't propose to make an arrest, yet.'

'Could he arrest the lady, sir?'

'He could detain her for questioning,' said Rollison. 'The truth is that he thinks he can get her whenever he wants and prefers to have an unanswerable case before doing so. He'll probably get some kind of story from Marcus Shayle. So, Jolly, more cause for gloom! Deep gloom, because Grice has done practically everything we hoped we would be able to do ourselves—my mind hasn't been working lately or we would have got this information first.'

'Perhaps so, sir,' said Jolly, unconvinced. 'What do you propose to do?'

'We are going to prove him wrong,' said Rollison. 'The little man with the knife and the footman at Barrington House are two people on whom we can check and Grice gave me some consolation; he's not very hopeful about East End contacts. I'll go there in the morning.'

'What about the—ah—Countess, sir?'

'You have not failed to notice,' said Rollison, 'that at our suggestion a policewoman is acting as her bodyguard. So the police are responsible for her. I'm not at all sure that Grice isn't holding his hand because of that. If anyone tries to get in touch with her, he'll learn at once. If she tried to slip away, the maid would stop her. On the other hand,' Rollison went on, stifling a yawn, 'there has been no crime in England of which she could have been guilty—as far as we know.'

'That is so,' said Jolly. 'Is there anything more, sir?' Rollison shook his head. 'What time shall I call you in the morning?'

'Nine o'clock should be about right,' said Rollison.

He was still asleep when Jolly came in next morning with the ornate silver tray, the post and the newspapers. It was half-past nine.

'The newspapers are not very informative this morning and there is no report of Miss Barrington-Ley's accident,' Jolly said.

'Pleasure for Pomeroy,' said Rollison.

He looked through the post; there was nothing of particular interest and he put it aside. Then he looked through *The Times* financial pages and frowned when he saw the closing prices. Many of the companies in which Barrington-Ley had an interest were showing a fall.

As he looked over the headlines of *The Record*, he wondered why that enterprising newspaper had not followed up the story of the Lady of Lost Memory. Then he saw a single column headline which Jolly had missed. It read:

CITY MYSTERY
WELL-KNOWN BANKER MISSING

Rollison read the story carefully. There was nothing in it that he did not know but it talked of rumours on the Stock Exchange and pointed to the fall in price of Barrington-Ley stock, hinted that Barrington-Ley had been acting in an unusual manner and finally said that he had not been seen nor heard of for at least forty-eight hours.

Rollison put the paper aside, shaved and breakfasted in a hurry and was soon on the way to Fleet Street.

Lila, Countess Hollern, if that was in fact her name, had not put in an appearance. In calmer mood, he could consider with more equanimity the possibility that she had succeeded in deceiving him completely. He remained unconvinced. He went over the events of the previous evening in his mind and, remembering her face when she had heard the National Anthem of her country, came to the firm conclusion that no one could have acted quite as well as that. Consequently he was in better spirits than he expected to be but he knew that the tempo of the case was quickening.

His taxi pulled up outside the office of *The Record*.

The editorial staff would not come in until the afternoon—but some of the reporters might be gathered in the news-room or the canteen, before starting out for their day's assignments. He found three of them in the canteen and was greeted with a cheerful invitation to a cup of coffee.

'And what brings the great Toff along at this ungodly hour?'

demanded a little red-faced man with a wrinkled nose and a wicked eye. He was a crime reporter of renown.

'They tell me he's been frustrated,' said a tall, middle-aged man with a scar on his right cheek. 'Perhaps he wants to become a newspaper man.'

'Not a hope,' said the third, the youngest of the trio. 'Not one hope this side of the Great Divide, Rolly—we wouldn't have you for a fortune!' He grinned and offered cigarettes and then passed a cup of coffee. 'Sandwich?'

'No, thanks,' said Rollison. He bent his eyes on the youngest. 'Teddy,' he said, 'I thought you would see that there was some life in *The Record*, but even you've disappointed me.'

'I resent that,' said the tall man.

'*The Record*,' said the little man, in a fruity voice, 'is always first with the news, first with the views, a lively, witty, reliable and always accurate reflection of the opinion of the people. For exposure of all rackets, try *The Record*. Proprietor's stated policy,' he added with a grin.

'There isn't much the matter with the blatt,' said the tall man, judicially. 'It's got its bad points but it's got a lot of good ones. What's your complaint, Rolly?'

'The Barrington-Ley *Bal Masque*,' said Rollison. 'Why didn't you follow it up?'

'We squeezed it dry,' said Teddy.

'One day was enough,' said the tall man.

'I don't know so much,' said the little man frowning. 'I see what you mean. Now we've come out with this story about Barrington-Ley. Is there a connection?'

'That's what I want to know,' said Rollison.

'Your interest being?' asked Teddy.

'Impersonal,' Rollison assured him.

Teddy laughed. 'What a hope!' He looked speculatively at the others. 'Where did the Barrington-Ley story come from last night? Ticky found it, didn't he?'

'Ticky?' echoed Rollison.

'T I Keller, City Editor,' said Teddy. 'He doesn't often give us pieces of fruit but he found something there.'

'Would he know that Barrington-Ley was missing?' asked Rollison.

'Now we're finding out what Rolly's after,' said Teddy, greatly pleased. 'Friend of yours?'

'In a manner of speaking,' said Rollison. 'And he has many other friends. Many will be on the war-path. That article amounts to defamation of character and whoever started it is likely to get into a serious jam unless he can prove that there's something in it. I don't look on *The Record* as an organ of unblemished reputation,' went on Rollison, 'but I thought a word of warning might not come amiss.'

All three looked concerned. *The Record*, with all its faults, was regarded affectionately by most of its staff and they would be concerned if there were any serious likelihood of trouble for anyone among them.

'Ticky's in, isn't he?' asked the tall man.

'Unless he's got his ear close to the ticker in the City,' said Teddy. 'Shall I go and see?'

'It might be a help,' said Rollison.

They went up to the next floor and along many narrow corridors until at last they reached a door on which was the name: T. I. KELLER. A squeaky voice invited them to enter.

Two girls were at small desks against one wall and a small, extremely well-dressed man with a rose in his button-hole was sitting at an enormous desk which was littered with papers. The tape-machine at his side was ticking away steadily but he was paying it no attention. A pair of bright, bird-like eyes surveyed the newcomers and a birdlike face showed some bewilderment at the sight of Rollison.

'I am *very* busy,' he said, in a falsetto voice. 'Very.'

'The age of miracles is about to dawn,' said Teddy. 'Pause for a moment, old chap. Here is Old Man Doom come to wave a shroud over your head—Mr Richard Rollison.'

Ticky whistled.

'I *thought* I had seen you before.'

Teddy grinned. 'What a newspaper! A member of the staff who thinks he knows The Toff! Rollison says you've pulled a boner about Barrington-Ley,' went on Teddy, 'and I thought I'd let you see and disabuse him. The old blatt is never wrong.' He winked and went out.

Keller did not look at him but at Rollison. He seemed worried, his eyes looked less bird-like and he dropped all the pose of too busy to see him.

'Are you serious?' he asked.

'The story isn't liked in certain quarters,' said Rollison, anticipating the truth, 'and there will be repercussions. Of course, if you can prove that he's missing, that's a different matter, although even then the comments about his companies are pretty broad.'

'Oh, they don't matter,' said Keller, squeaking. 'They're facts— you can find them on the City page of any newspaper. The other—' he pursed his thin lips. 'Are you from the family, by any chance?'

'They don't know I'm here,' said Rollison.

'Hmm. Well, to tell you the truth,' said Keller, confidentially, 'I got a little bit tiddly last night. Not a thing I do often,' he added, hastily. 'I shot a line or two about the Barrington-Ley business and a fat little chap who was in the 'Chameleon' got my ear. Breathed deep, dark secrets. Barrington-Ley missing from home, family greatly worried, you know the kind of thing. I checked here and there telephoned his country home and the London house, got evasive replies and it all seemed to tie up. The truth is,' said Keller, a little sadly, 'I ought to stick to the City. I always go outside when I've had one or two— subconscious longing, I suppose, I used to think I would make a good reporter. Er—seriously, will there be trouble?'

'If I were you I would build a good defence,' said Rollison.

'Oh, I will, I will! It's a good thing you warned me or I would have forgotten it,' said Keller. 'I wish I could think of the fat fellow's name. He did give it to me. Smith, I think.'

'Or Brown,' said Rollison, sardonically, 'or, by a great stretch of the imagination, Pomeroy.'

'It wasn't Pomeroy,' said Keller, decidedly. 'Nice little chap, very soft voice, looked like a butler.'

'Pointed chin with bags of flesh on either side?' asked Rollison.

'That's the man! Now I come to think of it,' said Keller, 'he was a bit anxious that I should know the whole truth. Usually they ask for a fiver for the story and we don't say no. He just wanted to dispense information. I say, *is* Barrington-Ley missing?'

'I shouldn't rely on it,' said Rollison. 'You can't recall the fat man's name, I suppose. Was it Shayle?'

'No,' said Keller, firmly. 'No, it was something more common-or-garden than that. Smith has it. Or, as you say, Brown. I *am* a damned

fool!' he added, shrilly. 'Still, forewarned and all that. Very nice of
you to come. I'll have a defence like reinforced concrete if the Old
Man asks me about it—and he will, he always does if there's anything
the slightest bit wrong. I say, old chap,' he added, with a sly look,
'you couldn't give me a pillar or two for the defence, could you? It's
your market, you know.'

Rollison said: 'What time did you put the story in?'

'Oh, half-past one or thereabouts, it missed the country editions.
That's a help, the Old Man's gone north, I think. Or was that yesterday?
Why?'

'There was an attempt to murder Miss Barrington-Ley before
midnight,' said Rollison. 'You could have heard rumours of that but
because you wouldn't put in anything you couldn't vouch for, you
didn't use that story. That would show perspicacity wouldn't it?'

'I say, that's pretty good!' said Keller, beaming. 'Miss B-L was
hurt, was she?'

'Yes. And if you have a word with Teddy and send him over to
Barrington House to make inquiries, it would round off your
defence,' said Rollison. 'Of course, that's only a suggestion.'

Rollison left the office, not dissatisfied. Before his righteous outburst
at Barrington House, Pomeroy had made sure that the newspapers knew
of Barrington-Ley's disappearance which was a curious fact, to say the
least. Here was confirmation, if it were wanted, that there was much
more behind the story than Grice suspected.

Rollison went to Aldgate by taxi, then took a bus along the Mile
End Road. The people and the traffic streamed by him and he felt
stirred by this contact with the East End which to so many looked drab
and to him looked so colourful. People whom he knew or had met
passed him, not knowing he was there, little crooks mixing with men
and women who were as strictly law-abiding as any in the country,
bookmakers perpetually warring with the police, professional pick-
pockets and bag-snatchers who spent half their time in prison and the
other half trying to keep out but who did not seem able to give up the
game. Here they thrived, amiable little people for the most part with
their own code of honour and a suspicion and dislike of the police
which ran side-by-side. Nine out of ten he passed would no more steal
or pick pockets than commit murder but when the police wanted

information about this man or that they were sphinx-like. In many ways a strange motley, with a mixture of all races, Jews and Gentiles shoulder to shoulder in a curious fraternising which so often led to many people, all self-righteous, drawing the wrong conclusions.

He almost forgot Lila, Countess Hollern and over-shot his stop, so that he had to walk back along the crowded pavements with trams clattering past him and shopkeepers' touts watching him hopefully, for the rich sometimes came to the East End to pick up 'bargains' and complained when they were disappointed. There were two sides to every bargain in the East End.

One thing was noticeable; no one seemed to recognise him. At one time he could not have walked along this thoroughfare without being noticed, spoken to, nodded at, pointed out and certainly scowled at ferociously. It was a reflection on the rarity of his visits of late.

At last he reached Bill Ebbutt's public house, behind which there was a gymnasium for Bill Ebbutt, a large man now running to fat, had been a boxer in his youth and still loved the sport. Chopping blocks and coming champions were nursed under his benevolent wing. Those who could afford to pay for training paid, those who could not were trained all the same and few failed to recompense Bill Ebbutt when they began to earn money.

There were only three people in the public bar and no one was behind it. The occupants looked up at Rollison and as quickly looked away. All were strangers to him and all were suspicious of a well-dressed man of Rollison's appearance in the bar.

Then Bill Ebbutt waddled behind the bar. His face was pale, his eyelids drooped, he looked tired—as he always did—and his little ears, delicate almost as a child's, were prominent only because he was nearly bald.

'Hallo, Bill,' said Rollison.

Bill looked up and his little mouth gaped. He raised both hands, kept staring, then broke into a smile which seemed to double the size of his mouth and brought his hands crashing down on the bar.

'Bless my 'eart an' soul, if it ain't Mr Ar! Well corlummee, if it ain't Mr Ar! Well, I never did!' He took Rollison's hand in his vast fingers and squeezed it. 'I never did!' he said, wheezing. 'I thought you'd deserted us, Mr Ar, ever since the curate business you 'aven't put your nose inside the place.* Good boy, that parson, though I say it myself—do you know what?'

'What?' asked Rollison, greatly pleased.

'My ole woman's deserted'the Army an' now she goes to church, that's a fack. Proper looks dahn on them brass-blowing buglers, she do, and her uniform—she just won't put it on. I bought 'er a n'Ancient an' Modern fer 'er birfday, you know, one wiv music, and she was as prahd as punch of it, proper prahd. Gets a bit monotonous singing 'ymns *every* night.' added Bill Ebbutt, 'but still, anythink for a quite life, I says.' He paused, and then burst out: 'Now what am I a-thinking of, Mr Ar—what'll you 'ave? The same?'

'The same.'

'Good old mild and bitter,' said Bill, taking a glass. 'I remember the first mild-and-bitter you 'ad in my 'ouse, Mr Ar, same as if it was yesterday. 'Ere, I'll tell you what—come into the parlour and meet the ole woman again. She'll be tickled to death to see you.' He wheezed in high good humour, and added: 'You know the way!'

Sitting in the parlour at the back of the pub, Bill Ebbutt regaled Rollison with the local gossip, hoped that he would soon be about more often, said that Mrs Bill would soon be in and then, when he seemed too breathless to talk any more, he leaned forward and said with a broad wink:

'What's on your mind, Mr Ar?'

Rollison laughed. 'You're a deep old scoundrel, Bill!'

'You didn't fink I fought you'd come to say 'ow are yer at this time o' day, did yer?' asked Bill, with a shake of his head. 'I know better'n that. If you'd come for that you would 'ave chose to-night when all the boys is abaht. Anythink much?'

'I don't yet know,' said Rollison. 'There was a little fellow picked up by the police last night or early this morning. Known to use a knife.'

'Larry Bingham,' said Bill promptly, and scowled. 'Nasty little piece o' work, that Bingham. I wouldn't raise a finger to 'elp 'im, Mr Ar, an' that's the truth. 'Ad a cut at a lady in the West End, didn't 'e?'

'So that's reached you,' said Rollison.

*The Toff And The Curate

'Cor strike a light, we don't miss much!' said Bill. 'Friend o' yours? The lady, I mean?'

'Yes.'

'Dirty little tyke,' said Bill and then showed some alarm. 'Larry, I means. Well, I dunno that I can 'elp yer much but I do know this. He owed Malloy a pony. Usually does a job to pay off 'is debts, Larry does, never got a penny to bless hisself wiv. You'd think a man would 'ave the common to lay off the racket when it don't show a divvy, wouldn't you, Mr Ar? I mean, I can understand a man keeping at the game if he's making a good fing aht of it, although I don't approve of it, mind you; I'm all for law and order. Malloy's been very flush lately,' he added.

'Do you know whom Malloy's working for?'

'No,' said Bill. 'He's a close one, he is, but I'll tell yer what— Percy Dann lives next door to Malloy, maybe he knows somethink. Should be in any time, 'e always 'as 'is pint before dinner, Percy does. Just a minute, Mr Ar, I'll go an' see if 'e's arrived.'

He came back in a few minutes, followed by a painfully thin and ugly man with a despondent face and dreary brown eyes and an Adam's apple which moved up and down above his choker. He wore an oily-looking cloth cap at the back of his head and in his right hand he carried a pint glass.

Bill said: 'Got 'im for yer, Mr Ar!'

'Coo lumme, look-oo-it-is,' said Percy Dann, running the words together as if he could not utter them fast enough. 'I-never-fought-I'd-live-ter-see-this-day Mister Ar. 'Ow are yer?'

He extended a limp hand.

He let it drop into Rollison's and then gripped-and had Rollison not known that Percy Dann, for all his thinness, had remarkably powerful fingers, he would have been taken by surprise. Percy had spent several years in prison for using those remarkable fingers in order to pick locks, for he was double-jointed and had great dexterity as well as strength in them. He had since retired and had succeeded in convincing the police that his only income now came from the little tobacconist's shop in a side street leading from the Mile End Road.

'How's Mrs Dann?' asked Rollison, and Bill gasped in dismay but could not prevent a five minutes' discourse on the troubles of Mrs Dann. She was not well. She had undergone two operations and the doctors didn't know what they were doing; doctors, Percy Dann wouldn't give a fiver for all the doctors in London; they had properly finished off his wife, they had, she was so weak she could hardly crawl about the shop. He began to go into some detail about the operations when Rollison asked him if he would have another.

'Why, sure, Mr Ar,' said Percy, and finished his glass in a single gulp. 'Same again, Bill. I was saying — '

'How's Malloy getting on these days?' asked Rollison, quickly.

'Oh, 'im,' said Percy, disparagingly. 'I never did like that perisher an' nor does the wife. Never will, neither. Why, lives next door to us, he does, an' do you think 'e made a single hinquiry about the wife when she 'ad 'er op? Not 'im. Didn't trouble to hinquire once, not even when she come back.'

'How's his business?' asked Rollison.

'Mighty suspicious, if you arst me,' said Percy darkly. ''E's got plenty of nickel, no questions asked. ''E'd put Larry Bingham up ter that job larst night, if you arst me. Lot o' coming and going there is, too. Why, if it ain't Bill wiv the goods,' he broke off and did justice to the second pint, after wishing The Toff good luck.

'Who has come and gone?' asked Rollison and, before Percy could launch into a monologue, added: 'Has there been a short, fat man who favours bright check suits?'

Percy looked at him shrewdly.

'Always on the mark, that's Mr Ar. You mean Ole Nosey.'

'Nosey?' repeated Rollison.

'S'right. I dunno 'is name, but 'e's a reg'lar visitor, 'as been for munce. Come along the road one day wiv a nose like a rear light — I remember it well because it was the day the wife come out, proper weak she was but when she saw 'is nose — laugh? She nearly died a' laughing! Said a man of 'is age ought a know better than look through keyholes, she did; 'e didn't arf give 'er a look. 'Ad it for weeks, that nose. Well, a week, anyway.'

'How long ago was this?' asked Rollison.

'Matter o' three or four weeks,' said Percy. 'The wife'll know, got a memory for dates, she 'as. Tell yer what,' added Percy, lowering his voice. 'Nosey was at Malloy's last night, he was, and so was Larry

Bingham. About eight o'clock, it was—what time did I get 'ere, Bill?'

'About eight,' said Bill.

'Then it musta been a bit before,' said Percy, 'I see them both, I did, I said to myself, they're up to a bit o' no good, they are. You can always tell. When Larry got knocked off, was I surprised? No, sir, you ask the wife. I told 'er, I said to 'er, there'll be trouble, Liz, you mark my words, Larry's been out a work too long. No, I wasn't surprised. Takes a lot to surprise me,' added Percy, darkly. 'You'd be surprised at what I know—wouldn't 'e, Bill?'

'S'right,' said Bill.

'I take a man for what he is,' went on Percy, 'never mind 'is business so long as 'e pays spot cash, no credit in my business, no more than there is in Bill's.' The thought amused him. 'Well,' he said when he had recovered, 'does it 'elp, Mr Ar?'

'A great deal,' said Rollison, warmly. 'Has Nosey been along this morning?'

'The wife never said so and there ain't much that misses the missus,' declared Percy and went off into another paroxysm of laughter. 'Malloy's at 'ome—'ad two telegrams, I can tell you that; I see the boy myself. If I knew what was in them telegrams,' added Percy, 'I could tell you a lot, that's a fact. Well I'd better get along, dinner'll be waiting and the wife likes me to 'ave it 'ot. Be seeing yer, Mr Ar.'

'You'll see me in ten minutes or so,' said Rollison, 'I'm coming to have a word with Mr Malloy.'

'Cor, lumme,' said Percy, 'some people don't arf like trouble, don't they, Bill? An' some works fast, I will say that fer you, Mr Ar, you don't let the grass grow in the medder! Why don't you come along o' me an' meet the missus?'

'I don't want you mixed up in this,' said Rollison.

'I dunno as I wants to be mixed up in it meself,' said Percy, frankly, 'but I don't mind lendin' you a n'and. Come to think,' he said, 'Malloy's been 'avin' some posh visitors lately. Made 'is wife mad, the wife says.'

Rollison said, quickly: 'Women?'

'There was one skirt,' said Percy. 'Little thing, wiv a nose aimin' at the sky. You know. Snub. All lad-di-dah.' Percy raised his voice an octave.   'Weally, Mrs Malloy, I'm only a *fwiend* of your *h*usband's.' He laughed at himself and added:

'Only worse, Mr Ar.'

'When was she last there?' asked Rollison, feeling quite sure that this visitor was Janice Armitage.

'S'matter of fact I think the wife said she was along there just before I come for me pint,' said Percy. 'I was at the back an' never see her. Tell yer what, Mr Ar—if she's there, I'll be in the winder of my shop. Okay?'

'I'll come five minutes after you,' said Rollison.

'Gimme ten,' said Percy, 'I got to 'ave me dinner. Then there was another skirt, I never see much of 'er. Come arter dark an' went aht arter dark.'

'Oh,' said Rollison, thoughtfully, and thought of Lady Lost. Percy could give no details except that he thought she had a fur coat.

'So long, thanks for the pint,' said Percy. He winked, offered his hand again and this time left it limp in Rollison's, and then walked out.

A quarter of an hour later, Rollison followed him.

CHAPTER FOURTEEN

Mr Malloy

THE STREET WHERE Percy Dann had his shop was long and narrow with small houses on either side—one of long lines of drab terraces. Here and there a house was freshly painted but the landlords of that particular street were not inclined to be generous with decorations.

Mr Malloy lived in one of the houses which had been freshly painted. Next door, the paint from the shop was peeling off, the showcards in the window were brown with age and freely fly-spotted, a few cartons had fallen down and were covered in dust and the window was still stuck with gummed paper as a protection against blast. Mr Malloy's windows, on the other hand, positively shone. The front door-step, which was flush with the pavement, was freshly whitened, the brass letter-box and brass knocker, particular to that house, glistened in the sunlight. It looked an oasis of respectability in a slough of disrepute—but the police as well as Rollison knew that little else about Mr Malloy was respectable.

No one knew exactly what he did for a living.

The police had never been able to take him to court and although Rollison had heard vague rumours about him, he had never met the man; he had, however, seen him at a distance. He remembered a small, middle-aged man with sparse black hair heavily oiled and plastered over his cranium, showing little streaks of pink, a flabby face and a drooping moustache, also dark but streaked with grey.

As Rollison drew near the house, which was Number 91, he saw a figure at the window of the shop next door and through the grime recognised Percy. At first he thought that Percy was beckoning him but when the thin man waved his hand he decided that he was sending him away. That might mean that Janice had left and suggested that Percy did not consider the moment ripe for a visit. Rollison motioned over his shoulder with his thumb, Percy shook his head vigorously and went through his former antics.

Then Rollison saw what he meant; he was weaving his forefinger about his nose; 'Nosey' was inside.

Rollison beamed his thanks and knocked heavily.

After a short pause a woman opened the door. She was dressed in dark blue, was neat and well made up without being pretty or looking cheap. Narrowed blue eyes looked Rollison up and down, before she said:

'Good morning.'

'Good morning,' said Rollison. 'I would like to see Mr Malloy.'

'On what business?' she asked.

'Strictly private business,' said Rollison.

'He is engaged.'

'Tell him to see me at once or the police will be here within half an hour,' said Rollison.

The threat did not appear to frighten her but it did make her narrow her eyes still more; they were curiously hooded, the lids thick and jutting out a little at each side of her eyes.

'You'd better come in,' she said.

She stood aside for Rollison to enter a narrow passage. A light was on above the stairs, otherwise the hall and narrow staircase would have looked dark. The walls were freshly distempered and the paint was fresh green—it reminded him of Phyllis Armitage at Leeming House. Hardly had the thought crossed his mind than the woman had passed him to enter a room on the right. Then he heard a familiar, feminine voice.

'I really don't see what you mean.'

'Well, well!' murmured Rollison. 'Sister Janice *is* on the scene again.' He could not hear what the woman said but a man's harsh voice was raised immediately afterwards.

'What is he like?'

The woman described Rollison so well that he silently congratulated her.

'Rollison!' exclaimed Pomeroy, his voice no longer soft and gentle.

'That b...' said Malloy.

'Why, that seems like Mr Rollison!' declared Janice. She sounded greatly relieved.

'Be quiet, you little fool!' snapped Malloy. 'Flo, take her next door.'

Janice exclaimed: 'I won't go next door!'

Her words were stopped abruptly; there was a sound which might have been the result of a blow across the face. Rollison turned the handle and flung the door open.

Half-way across the room, moving towards a door which presumably led to the back of the house, was Janice Armitage. Her neck was bent forward, her shoulders were against Malloy's chest; he had his hands beneath her arm-pits and was dragging her with her heels sliding along the floor. The woman named Flo was opening the door and Pomeroy was standing against a bookcase, looking thoroughly alarmed.

'Good afternoon,' said Rollison. 'How much is the entertainment tax?'

Malloy dropped the girl; her head struck his thighs, his shins and then the floor. He swung round on his heel, flinging words at Flo.

'Get out, fetch Mike, tell Barney.'

Rollison said: 'Stay here, forget Mike, ignore Barney.'

'Get going!' screamed Malloy.

The woman stood by the door as if she were deliberately defying Malloy, whose flabby face was stained red. Pomeroy was still standing by the bookcase. He appeared to have recovered from the shock and his right hand was moving slowly towards his pocket. Rollison saw a vase filled with artificial flowers on a table by his side. He picked up the vase and tossed it towards Pomeroy, saying:

'Catch!'

The man dodged to one side and came nearer Rollison who rounded the table, took Pomeroy's right arm and held it high above his head, keeping the man on a stretch. He put his hand into the pocket and drew out an automatic; he dropped Pomeroy, who collapsed in a heap on the floor.

Malloy struck the woman across the face, a resounding blow which sent her reeling against the wall and then he swung round on Rollison. He also had a gun. They appeared to level the guns at the same moment—and neither fired. For a moment there was silence, as if the room had become a vacuum. Then it was broken by a gasping sound from Pomeroy, who began to get to his feet.

'Sit down,' Rollison said to him and Pomeroy collapsed into a chair. 'Malloy, put that gun away.'

If Malloy decided to shoot, he was not likely to miss. Rollison watched his gun-hand, wondering if he could judge the moment when the finger moved on the trigger. Then he saw Flo, who had been leaning against the wall with her hands covering her face, peering between the fingers. She moved, startling him enough to make him swing round towards her, but she struck at Malloy's arm and knocked the gun out of his grasp.

'You crazy fool!' she blazed.

Malloy, beside himself, turned on her. She struck out at at him but before Rollison could reach the man he had caught her hair and pulled her towards him, forcing her down on her knees. Then Rollison struck Malloy on the side of the head with the butt of Pomeroy's gun. Malloy did not even gasp. His fingers lost their grip, he staggered to one side and pitched down, lying across Janice's legs.

'Aren't we having a time?' said Rollison.

The woman was pushing the hair out of her eyes. She looked sullenly at Rollison and then at Malloy and she was breathing heavily. Pomeroy was gasping for breath, as if the vicarious action had affected him. He was sitting like a little fat ball in a small armchair.

The woman said: 'What do you want?'

'I wanted a talk with Mr Malloy,' said Rollison, 'but I shall need more now. Is the girl hurt?'

'No more than he is.'

'I hope you're right. Who are you?'

'Mrs Malloy,' she said.

'Not very loyal,' murmured Rollison.

'Do you think I want to see him hanged?' she flared.

'No,' said Rollison, slowly, 'nor do you want to be hanged with him. Where are Mike and Barney?'

'Along the street.'

'Are they likely to come here in the next half hour?'

'Not unless they're sent for,' she said.

'I hope that's true, too,' said Rollison and looked down as Malloy stirred. 'Help him into a chair and then put the girl on the settee.' He turned to Pomeroy and his voice grew sharp. 'So we haven't met before, Pomeroy?'

The man said nothing but licked his lips.

Rollison said: 'You employed Larry Bingham, through Malloy, to attack Gwen Barrington-Ley and then you spread the story of Barrington-Ley being missing.'

Pomeroy said: 'I didn't know Bingham would use a knife.'

'Perhaps you prefer poison *à la* Countess,' said Rollison.

He needed no further proof that the Lady of Lost Memory was known to some people as the Countess.

This was a different Pomeroy from the man at Barrington House, because he was frightened. His eyes opened, his mouth gaped; his nerve was completely gone.

'You–*know*–her!'

'Shut your damned mouth,' said Malloy.

He was sitting forward in his chair, looked dazed and there was a trickle of blood from the side of his head. It ran down to his chin and disappeared under his collar. He was glaring at Pomeroy and suddenly he changed the direction of his gaze and looked at his wife. Malignance indescribable was in his eyes and he began to swear at her and she at him, both vitriolic, obscene.

On the settee, Janice Armitage did not stir.

Rollison looked round for a telephone but could not see one. He might make Percy Dann hear, if he called, but a shout would be as likely to attract someone passing by and an appeal for the police would be ignored, might even bring aid to the wrong side.

He could wait until Janice came round, he decided, and meanwhile he could question Pomeroy, now staring apprehensively at the Malloys, whose flood of abuse was slackening. The woman fell silent but continued to glare at her husband.

Rollison said: 'We'll have the full story now, Pomeroy.'

Malloy swung round. 'Keep your mouth shut!'

'*Now*, I said,' said Rollison.

Pomeroy was as much afraid of Malloy as of him and licked his lips but remained silent. Then Janice stirred; it should not be long before she was able to go for help.

Flo Malloy said: '*I'll* tell you, these damned fools don't know when they're beaten. Listen, Rollison, I—'

She backed away when Malloy rose to his feet. The man looked as if he would defy Rollison and the gun and actually stepped towards her. For the first time Rollison saw that the woman was frightened.

The glare did what oaths could not and she shrugged her shoulders and looked away from him with her lips tightly set.

'Don't change your mind,' said Rollison to her.

'It's changed for her,' said Malloy, turning towards him with a sneer. 'You think you're clever, don't you—well, you'll learn different. If you knew everything we could tell you, you still wouldn't know much. If you want to know the *whole* story, find the Countess, she'll tell you.'

Rollison said: 'What Countess?'

'I thought you knew all about her,' said Malloy, 'and *you* thought I was unconscious.' He looked at Pomeroy. 'He's all gas, he doesn't know a thing.'

That was the moment when they heard a sound inside the house.

Malloy moved his head round quickly and Pomeroy clapped his hands together as if in anguish. Rollison whispered:

'Quiet—all of you.'

Malloy opened his lips and then caught sight of the gun and discretion triumphed. Flo stared at the door which still stood ajar. Pomeroy was uttering little noises in his throat but they were not loud enough to be heard outside.

'Malloy, where are you?' There were heavy footsteps in the next room, a smothered oath and then: 'You've got to get out, the police are coming!'

A man came into the room.

Rollison stared incredulously at Marcus Shayle who stood, quite as dumbfounded, on the threshold of the room.

CHAPTER FIFTEEN

Hue And Cry

MALLOY TOOK FULL advantage of the opportunity that offered. Looking round as Shayle paused, he saw that Rollison's gun was pointing towards the door and that Rollison was momentarily off his guard. He put his hands beneath the edge of the table and tipped it up and as Rollison realised the danger the table struck him on the thigh. As he staggered against the wall he remembered Malloy's gun and tried desperately to regain his balance.

'Snap into it!' Malloy shouted.

Pomeroy bounded from the chair, jumped past Rollison and sped into the passage while Marcus Shayle turned back and disappeared. For an agonising moment Malloy and his wife stared at each other; then Malloy moved towards the gun.

Flo bent down, snatched it up and flung it through the window. There was a crash of breaking glass. Loud footsteps sounded in the street and then grew fainter. From inside the house Shayle shouted:

'Don't waste time!'

'If you breathe a word,' Malloy said to his wife. 'I won't rest until I've killed you.' There was no passion in his voice, it was a simple statement of intention. Then he went out of the door into the next room.

The front room was curiously quiet. The woman stood against the wall with her hands at her face and Janice stirred again but did not open her eyes. Rollison tried the door into the next room but found it locked. He went into the street but there was no sign of Pomeroy. As he turned back into the little house, the door of the shop opened and Percy appeared, his Adam's apple working at lightning speed.

'S'matter?' he demanded, shrill-voiced.

'Most of the birds have flown,' said Rollison.

'Cor-lumme, you didn't *start* anything!'

'Not enough,' said Rollison. 'The police will be here any moment, Percy, I shouldn't stay if you don't want to be a witness.'

'What, me?' said Percy.

He went back into his shop and Rollison looked along the street.

Two cars were coming round the corner. He shrugged his shoulders resignedly as he went into the front room. Mrs Malloy had not moved but she had taken her hands from her face and was staring at Janice, whose eyes were open and who looked bewilderedly about her. She saw Rollison and tried to get to her feet but dropped back with a gasp and said plaintively:

'Oh, my head is *terrible*.'

'Just sit still,' said Rollison.

The cars pulled up outside and he met Grice on the front doorstep. It was a harassed Grice with two sergeants who looked at Rollison in surprise.

'Are they here?' Grice demanded.

'No,' said Rollison.

'So you frightened them away.'

Rollison put his hand on the other man's shoulder.

'A man who should be under arrest warned them. The gang would have been waiting here for you if he hadn't arrived.'

Grice said slowly: 'So Shayle came here.'

'Yes.'

'He broke away from the two men who brought him up from Devon,' said Grice. 'That was at Waterloo, less than an hour ago, so he must have come straight here.'

'He warned them that the police were coming,' repeated Rollison.

'He gave this address when he cracked under questioning early this morning and afterwards regretted it,' said Grice. 'Have we got anything on Malloy?'

'Yes. Assault and battery at the very least.'

'Good!' said Grice. 'Was anyone else here besides Malloy and his wife?'

'A certain sporting gentleman who calls himself Pomeroy.'

'So he *is* in it.'

'Of course he's in it,' said Rollison. 'You're assuming that Malloy's wife went with them, aren't you? She preferred to stay behind and, but for her—' He smiled but without much humour. 'I'll give her my thanks in person,' he went on.

Grice made no comment and they went into the front room as two plainclothes policemen came through the other door, having gained entry through the kitchen. Mrs Malloy was still standing by the wall and when Grice approached her she looked at him steadily and said:

'I know nothing and I shall say nothing and all the police in London won't make me.'

'We'll see about that,' said Grice.

'And all the Superintendents, too,' she said, but there was no spirit in her and she dragged herself away from the wall to sit down on the arm of a chair.

Grice said slowly: 'Mrs Malloy, I don't want—'

'Steady old chap,' said Rollison, 'she's had a rough passage.' He saw the woman look at him in surprise. He then went to Janice's side. Janice was pressing her hands against her forehead and complaining about a headache. Rollison felt no particular sympathy towards her. Grice said that he was going to take them both to Scotland Yard for questioning. Janice turned to Rollison with tears in her eyes and begged him not to let them but he did not want to prevent the police from interrogating her.

Grice left a sergeant and a detective-officer to search the house, after Rollison had given him a detailed account of what had happened. Rollison particularly liked Grice's manner with Flo Malloy; he no longer tried to use the heavy hand but helped her into the police car where she sat next to Janice. Janice, knowing that she could not save herself from this indignity, sat in petrified silence.

Rollison sat next to Grice who followed the leading car towards the main road.

'Was the Malloy quarrel genuine?' he asked.

'Yes. Malloy would have done murder and his wife wanted to save him and probably herself from hanging,' said Rollison, 'but I doubt whether she will talk now. If you had seen the way the man looked at her you would understand why.'

'Looked?' Grice was sceptical.

'I hope he'll demonstrate for you one day,' said Rollison. 'Well, there we are and we can't do a great deal about it, except start a hue-and-cry.'

'That won't take long,' said Grice.

At Scotland Yard he put out a general call for all three missing men. The two women were left in a waiting-room, with a policeman in with them and another outside the door, while Grice put the instructions through from his office and then telephoned a report to the Assistant Commissioner. When he had finished, he leaned back in his chair and said:

'At least it was the Devon fellows who let Shayle go, we didn't. He buttered them into letting him walk without handcuffs.'

'When did you know that he had talked of Malloy?' asked Rollison.

'Not until I knew that he'd got away,' said Grice. 'The Devon fellows were so proud of having got something out of him that they said nothing in their telephoned report—they wanted to come and tell us how well they had done our job. Still, moaning about them won't help. How did you get on to Malloy?'

'It was general knowledge that Larry Bingham owed him fifty pounds,' said Rollison, 'and Larry has the reputation of paying his debts in kind. Larry was seen at the house yesterday afternoon.'

'You could have telephoned me,' said Grice, without much spirit.

'Yes, couldn't I?' said Rollison. 'I also heard that Janice Armitage was there and I didn't want to take chances with her.' He sat back.

Then: 'Did you get any information about your Countess?' Grice demanded.

'Your Countess—my unknown lady,' Rollison corrected.

'So you're sticking to that?'

'Firmly,' Rollison assured him. 'What's more, there is a chance that Lady Lost was at Malloy's house for a while.'

'Where did you hear that?'

'From chance remarks,' said Rollison.

Grice raised no objection to Rollison being present while he questioned the women. He chose Mrs Malloy first, believing that the longer Janice was on tenterhooks, the more readily she would talk.

Mrs Malloy refused to speak, refused to admit that her husband had struck Janice or her, and remained tight-lipped, looking sullenly at Grice with her curiously-lidded eyes half-narrowed. She denied the presence of any other woman at the house.

'All right,' Grice said. 'I'll see you again later.'

She turned to go with a man on either side of her.

'Flo,' said Rollison, as she reached the door.

She ignored him.

'Flo,' repeated Rollison, going across and looking into her eyes. 'Malloy isn't worth it. There'll never be a future for you with him again. Although you tried to stop him from doing murder, he will probably be hanged. Don't make it worse for yourself than it is now. If your worry is money, there are ways and means of helping.'

'I don't want your help,' Flo said.

'You may do, later.' He turned back into the room.

'You're fancying different types, aren't you?' said Grice.

'Don't be coarse,' said Rollison.

'Flo Malloy is as hard a nut as her husband,' said Grice. 'I felt sorry for her at the house, because of what he'd said and done, but I shouldn't be soft-hearted over her.'

Rollison made no comment.

When Janice came up she was in tears and it took all Grice's patience to coax the story out of her. She had been given Malloy's address by Marcus Shayle and had often been to the house—it was there that she received the "presents" he had sent her. She declared that she was desperately in love with Marcus and would do anything to help him and she didn't flinch when Grice talked of murder but she did make a comment surprisingly shrewd for her.

'No one's dead *yet.*'

'Why did you go there to-day?' demanded Grice.

She sniffed and dabbed at her red-rimmed eyes; she looked girlish and might have appealed to the sympathy of some men at the Yard but Grice was never impressed by tears or innocent looks. Eventually she told him that Pomeroy had sent for her and told her that Marcus would be released and that she would be able to see him if she went there that morning.

'And what happened when you got there?' demanded Grice.

She gulped. 'I—they—I mean Malloy, he said I was to—to go to Mr Rollison's flat!' She flung the words out defiantly and then added, tearfully: 'He wanted me to get the Countess away; he said it was important, he wanted me to distract Mr Rollison's attention, he said he could look after the rest. And I was to get a key of the flat if I could—I don't know what he thought I was!'

'Obviously he thought you were a friend of Mr Rollison,' said Grice.

She simpered. 'Well, I *am*, aren't I?'

Grice kept a straight face with difficulty and Rollison agreed bravely that she was. This gave the girl more confidence and Grice handled her well. The dress she was wearing might have come straight from a Paris *salon*, her shoes and gloves were of first quality and her hair looked as if it had been dressed by an artist only that morning.

Grice finished his questioning at last and Janice asked in her most little-girl voice:

'Have I satisfied you, Superintendent? *Please* say that I have. I wouldn't do anything that Malloy wanted me to if it would hurt a *fly*, I wouldn't reely.'

Grice's voice hardened.

'You were very wrong not to tell the police your fiancé's address, Miss Armitage—had you given us the information earlier, a great deal of trouble might have been prevented.'

'Well'—she paused—'you couldn't expect—I mean, you can't expect a *man* to know how I feel about Marcus, can you?'

Grice gave her up but still spoke with a severe voice.

'I must warn you, Miss Armitage, that if you get any further information about any of them—Marcus Shayle, Malloy or the man called Pomeroy, you must tell us immediately. If you have a letter or a postcard, with an address or without, you must not lose a moment in telling us. If you do, you may cause even more serious trouble for your fiancé.'

'Would I?' asked Janice.

'You see,' said Grice, carefully, 'it is by no means certain that Marcus Shayle is acting like this because he wants to. The others probably have some influence over him. It will be for his own good if he is found again. Do you understand me?'

There was a calculating look in her eyes.

'Yes,' she said, 'I didn't think of that before, I *am* sorry. If I have only a teeny-weeny note or even a telephone call I will tell you right away, that's a promise. Can I go now?'

'I will send a man home with you,' said Grice, pressing a bell. When a policeman in uniform entered, he told the man to take Janice to the waiting-room and arrange for her to be taken home.

'Right-ho, sir. Come along, Miss.' The constable took Janice out, not before she had looked at Rollison beneath her lashes with a glance which she doubtless thought was alluring.

When the door closed behind her, both of them laughed.

'You've an impressive circle of friends,' said Grice. 'Her type is as common as mud. She knew something of what was going on and, provided she came out of it well, she didn't greatly mind. Shayle must be fond of her or he wouldn't lavish so much money on her.'

'Or,' said Rollison.

Grice frowned. 'Or what?'

'Or else he felt it wise to lavish clothes on her to make sure that she kept her mouth shut,' said Rollison. 'Perhaps there is more than fluff in that funny little head of hers. That's only a suggestion, of course, and I may be quite wrong.' He offered cigarettes and, when Grice refused, lit one himself. 'You'll have her watched, won't you?'

'Of course,' said Grice. He sat back and smiled, although his expression was grave and he seemed concerned. 'Well, what about the Countess?'

'I'm a long way from convinced that she is a Countess, or even if she is, that she's half as bad as she's been painted,' said Rollison.

'It isn't like you to be so biased.'

'I'm judging from what I know of her. Bill, you started to base your case against her on the fact that she did not recognise certain tunes when they were played to her at the nursing home. That's pretty thin.'

'It was an idea, no more,' said Grice, 'and the rest developed directly from that. I've had a report in from the New York police,' he added, and took a telegram from his desk. 'Read it, it might help to convince you.'

There was confirmation of the amount of money that had been raised by Countess Lila Hollern and of the fact that it was in her bank, under her name, and without a joint signature. There was also the admission that well-known members of New York banking circles and society had vouched for her but a comment suggested that it might have been because of her looks. There was no doubt at all that the New York police considered that she had defrauded the public. The cable ended with the statement that action was being considered in New York and the hope that, if it materialised, Scotland Yard would be able to arrange for the Countess's extradition.

Rollison put down the cablegram and said slowly:

'Will you oblige them?'

'Not on the present evidence,' said Grice. 'In any case I doubt whether the Home Office would agree—we've plenty to discuss with the lady over here!'

'When are you going to start?'

'When I know a little more,' said Grice. 'Now, you've something on your mind—what is it?'

'Until she heard it in my flat, I don't believe that she had the Yugoslav National Anthem played to her,' said Rollison, quietly. 'I don't believe the matron carried out the instructions and I believe she gave a false report.'

'You're dreaming this up,' said Grice.

'Well, will you look into it?' asked Rollison.

After a pause, Grice said: 'All right.'

'Don't forget the police have made some errors in this case,' Rollison said. 'First they let Lady Lost go from the nursing home.'

'I've learned, since,' said Grice. 'A visitor in a fur coat went in— and, naturally, when my men saw a fur coat come out, they had no suspicions. Later they saw another fur coat, asked the wearer questions and then realised they had been tricked.'

The telephone rang as he finished.

'Grice speaking,' said Grice, into it. Rollison watched and saw his expression change, the skin grew tauter over his nose and cheeks and while still listening he pressed a bell-push on the desk. At last he said: 'Yes, stay there, touch nothing and move nothing and allow no one else in the room.

'If necessary lock the door, I will take the responsibility.' He replaced the receiver after a terse good-bye and looked grimly at Rollison as a constable answered his summons.

Grice said: 'Ask Chief Inspector Bernay to come in at once, then find out whether Sergeant Gorring is free. Tell the sergeant, if you find him, that we shall want everything for a case of homicide. He is to telephone Dr Gray. Failing Sergeant Gorring, get Sergeant Anderson.'

'Yes, sir,' said the constable, as if Grice had asked for a sandwich, and turned and went out.

'Homicide,' murmured Rollison.

'If Phyllis Armitage told me the truth just now, murder,' said Grice, getting up. 'I must pop upstairs and have a word with the Assistant Commissioner before I go. Are you coming?'

'Where?' asked Rollison.

'To the Lawley Nursing Home,' said Grice. 'Miss Armitage went to see the matron and found that she has been killed.' He paused by the door, looked at Rollison thoughtfully and then said with feeling: 'There are times when you're so uncanny that you scare me.'

Rollison said: 'Uncanny? I simply look at the facts. I'll see you there later,' he added, picking up his hat. 'I'm going to Barrington House first.'

CHAPTER SIXTEEN

Talk With Gwendoline

ROLLISON TOOK THE lift to the ground floor and hurried towards the exit, then doubled across the courtyard, to the surprise of several policemen. He turned towards Parliament Square, beckoned a taxi which was approaching and when the cab slowed up, he said: 'Wait for me outside the telephone kiosk round the corner—we're going to Park Lane.'

'Okay,' said the driver.

There was no delay when Rollison telephoned Jolly.

'Is there anything to report there?'

'No, sir. Our guest went for a short walk with her maid and they are now both back at the flat.'

'Good. Jolly, go to the Lawley Nursing Home quickly. Don't let the police know that I sent you, if you should be seen by them—say you were curious about the matron or something like that. Miss Phyllis Armitage is there—presumably in the matron's office. She has had instructions to keep everyone out, so go to the window and try to talk to her. Get her story if it's possible and then report to the flat. If I'm not there, telephone Barrington House.'

'Very good, sir,' said Jolly.

'Get a move on, Jolly!' Rollison rang off and hurried to the taxi. There was no sign of Grice's car as he passed the Yard. He sat back, lighting a cigarette. There was surely no further doubt that the matron had played a part in what had happened earlier. The trouble was to find out how Shayle, Pomeroy or Malloy had known that the Lady of Lost Memory would be put under her charge.

'Wait, will you?' he asked the taxi driver when they drew up outside Barrington House. 'I may be half an hour.' He was already walking towards the front door as he finished speaking and noticed with some surprise that the front gates were closed, preventing the taxi from going right in.

The footman, Farrow, opened the door.

'Good afternoon, sir.'

'Good afternoon,' said Rollison. 'Is Miss Gwendoline in?'

'No, sir, she is not at home.' Farrow looked as if he were glad to say so.

'Mrs Barrington-Ley?' asked Rollison.

'I am sorry, sir, but Madam is unwell and unable to receive anyone.'

'Take her my card,' Rollison said, taking one from his pocket.

'I am sorry, sir,' said the footman, firmly. 'The doctor was most emphatic—Madam is not to be disturbed. Madam was taken ill early this morning.'

'Is she unconscious?' demanded Rollison.

'I have no information, sir, beyond my instructions.'

'When did Miss Gwendoline go out?'

'I have no idea, sir.'

As he spoke the door of a room off the hall opened and a maid appeared. Before the door closed Rollison heard Gwendoline's voice:

'Tell him that he must come within an hour.'

'Very good, Miss,' said the maid.

Rollison strode past the footman, smiled at the maid and reached the door. Farrow came after him and, when Rollison turned suddenly, he saw the man's face set in alarm. The man actually stretched out an arm to stop him but drew back when Rollison said sharply:

'Don't ask for trouble!'

He was uneasily aware of the man's tense gaze when he went into the room. But for the urgency of seeing Gwendoline, he would have paid Farrow more attention for he had an impression that the man wanted to speak.

The morning-room was bright and sunny with books in the corners and a small writing-desk, small easy chairs dotted about and a low-sprung settee on which Gwendoline was sitting. She sat up abruptly when she saw him and showed no sign of pleasure.

'I told Farrow that I was not at home.'

'And Farrow told me,' said Rollison. He closed the door, walked across and stared at Gwendoline. She looked as if she had had no sleep the previous night. Her eyes were bright and glassy and her face was pale, the cheeks puffy beneath her eyes—obviously she had been crying. Her neck was heavily bandaged. Her hair was in disarray and her tweed suit was crumpled. Cigarette ash covered the lapels and her skirt and she looked almost disreputable.

'What is it now?' asked Rollison. 'And why aren't you in bed?'

'It was only a scratch,' she said. 'My neck is stiff, that's all. I don't want to see you—I don't want to see anyone.' Her voice was shrill with emotion.

'Have you been out this morning?' Rollison asked.

'No, I've been here all day.'

'Can you prove that?'

He stirred her to interest. She frowned and then stretched out for a cigarette in a box by her side. Her fingers were stained brown with nicotine.

'If necessary, yes.'

'Has your mother been out?'

'No, she —' She stood up quickly, wincing when she moved her head carelessly. 'She had a heart attack this morning. I thought she was going to die. I think Andrew saved her life.' She looked a picture of despair as she stood there with the unlighted cigarette dangling from her lips and her complexion rather muddy—never had Rollison seen Gwen Barrington-Ley looking so unattractive.

He said, quietly: 'What brought the attack on?'

'*I* don't know,' said Gwendoline and then she flared up. 'Why do you stand there asking questions? We asked you to help us and all you did was to tell the police and let yourself be fooled by that damned woman! I thought you were a *friend*!'

'You make it very difficult for your friends to help you,' said Rollison, gently. 'That doesn't mean that they don't want to. Gwen, were you speaking the truth when you told me that you had seen the woman at your father's office?'

'Yes!'

'Did you see them together?'

'No,' she said, 'she was waiting for him.'

'So other members of the staff must have seen her.'

'I thought you were a detective,' she said, sneering; that was not like Gwen. 'It was his private office—there is an entrance from the street, leading to a small waiting-room, and anyone with a key can get in—*anyone with a key*. She had that key, do you understand? She had a key which I have never been allowed to use, even mother had never had one. That whore—'

'Steady, Gwen.'

She flared up. 'Steady, steady, steady! I tell you she's a high-class tart, there isn't anything to be said in her favour; I wouldn't be surprised if she is behind all this!'

'All what?' asked Rollison.

'This dreadful violence! David's disappearance. The attack on me and the at—' She broke off, putting a hand to her lips, and then added in a quieter voice 'and everything.'

'And the attack on your mother,' murmured Rollison.

She tried to stare him out and failed. She tried to speak but the words would not come. She was afraid.

'So Hilda was attacked,' he said. 'Were you sending for Renfrew just now?'

She did not speak.

'You'll have to speak sooner or later,' said Rollison, 'you can't keep it secret for ever. Gwen, what has made you behave like this? What has made a man like Renfrew stake his reputation on concealing from the police an attempt on your mother's life? That *is* what happened, isn't it?'

She said: 'Damn you, yes.'

Rollison turned away and looked out of the window where the grass was fresh and bright and a rose walk was ablaze with colour. It was a pleasant, peaceful scene and the hum of traffic from Park Lane seemed remote from this seclusion!

'Gwen,' said Rollison, 'if this comes out, and it probably will, Renfrew will almost certainly have his name removed from the register. He may never be able to practise again. I'm told that he's a brilliant doctor and I'm also told that he's in love with you.'

'You shouldn't believe all you hear,' Gwendoline said in a muffled voice. 'Talking won't help, you can't help, you lost your chance. Please go away.'

'There is too much at stake,' said Rollison.

'All you can think about is that woman!'

'And you and your mother, David, and several other people dragged into the affair, into danger and perhaps to disaster, through no fault of their own,' said Rollison. 'Renfrew is one of them.' He hammered at that.

'Don't keep harping on Andrew!' Gwen cried.

Rollison said: 'There has been an attempt on your life, now on your mother's, your father is missing and may be dead, the matron of the Lawley Nursing Home has been murdered—'

Gwendoline screamed: 'No! No!'

'In cold blood, not very long ago,' said Rollison.

Gwen stood up slowly, moving as if her limbs were operated mechanically. She took out a lighter and lit her cigarette, staring at him all the time. The room was very quiet.

'Who was the matron?' Rollison asked, gently.

'Is there—is there no hope for her?' Gwendoline asked.

'None,' said Rollison.

Gwendoline stepped to the window and looked out. Her eyes were half-closed and looked too hot for tears. The cigarette drooped from her lips and smoke curved upwards, making her close one eye completely.

She said: 'That matron is—was—a lifelong friend of mother's. Mother financed the nursing home. David knew about it.' Her voice was low-pitched and monotonous. 'Then someone found out. Pomeroy. I don't know what influence he has over father but he persuaded father to let the nursing home be used for—for people who were not ill. People who were supposed to be "resting." I don't know a great deal about it, except that father was uneasy. Violet—the matron—frequently protested but there was nothing we could do; father insisted. Once or twice we knew that men or women wanted by the police were there under assumed names. It seemed madness but—father impressed it upon us that we must not tell the police or make difficulties. So we let it go on.'

She paused, but Rollison did not interrupt.

'It has been happening for over a year now,' said Gwendoline, drearily. 'It has been a constant source of anxiety but the real worry has been David. Why did he let this man tell him what to do? If it were known that a man in his position was doing such things, it would ruin him. We were constantly afraid and, although he pretended that there was nothing to worry about, we knew that he was desperately

worried. We tried to find out why but couldn't. It started from the
time that Pomeroy came to see him. Many queer things happened
from that time onwards. He transferred some of his business to
Pomeroy, Ward & Pomeroy. He used them as the accountants and
solicitors for the various charities which mother—mother tries to help.
It didn't seem to matter what Pomeroy wanted, he let them have their
own way. I think they know where he is now.'

Into a pause, Rollison said:

'Pomeroy made you keep away from me, didn't he?'

'Yes.'

'Why did you obey him?'

'Isn't it obvious? We were afraid for father—we did not know what
harm Pomeroy could do. And now Vi is dead, there will be an
inquiry, everything will come out.'

'Are you sure that you don't know what?' demanded Rollison.

'Yes,' she said. 'Yes, I'm not lying now. There is no point in lying.
The police will find out what happened at the nursing home, they will
learn that mother financed it, they will ask questions—questions—
questions! I've hated the sight of a policeman since this happened,
I've hated the sight and mention of them!'

'The police will do nothing that isn't necessary and won't rake up
muck for the sake of it. If a thing is done under coercion, the police
don't take such a serious view. That is, for crimes short of murder.
Have there been any mysterious deaths at the nursing home?'

'No,' Gwen said, and then added almost inaudibly: 'You know
what violence there has been.'

'You mean the attempt to kill the mystery lady?'

'Yes.'

'Did you know about it beforehand?' he asked, gently.

'I haven't sunk as low as that,' she said. 'No, but I knew afterwards
that Pomeroy was aware of it. I heard Pomeroy talking to someone on
the telephone. He had arranged that a new nurse, Armitage, should be
engaged—that was done through father's influence. I didn't hear all
the conversation but I gathered that she was to be blamed for it. He
had some particular reason for that, I don't know what it was.' She
turned and looked at him steadily. 'If she had been arrested I would
have told you, if not the police. Mother and I were quite determined

but when she was not affected, we did nothing. It seemed as if the police discovered the man who did it—did they?'

'Yes,' said Rollison. 'His name was Shayle, Marcus Shayle.' When Gwen showed no interest, he went on: 'A man of about twenty-seven or eight, pleasant-looking, with a round face and fair, curly hair. Does that sound familiar?'

'No,' said Gwen.

'You've never seen such a man with Pomeroy?'

'No.'

'All you know about that, then, is that Pomeroy wanted the woman dead and also arranged, or tried to arrange, that someone else should be found guilty of her murder,' said Rollison. 'You didn't get any indication of the reason why he wanted that done?'

'No.'

'Gwen,' said Rollison, after a pause, 'you have shown that you hate this woman and you knew that someone wanted to murder her. If this story comes out, and it may well do so, it might be thought that you condoned it. You haven't yet told me why you hate her so much. You must.'

'And then you will go and tell the police.'

'I shall tell them nothing unless I know it will save life,' said Rollison.

She looked at him very steadily, before she said.

'Pomeroy always talked of her as the Countess. I hate Pomeroy more than I thought it possible to hate anyone! I heard him planning to have the Countess arrive here, pretend to be suffering from loss of memory and be taken into the Nursing Home.'

'And then you heard him rejoice in the attempt to murder her.'

She said: '*Are* you a fool? It wasn't really an attempt, I thought it was at first but it wasn't. She was made ill but that was only so that she should win our sympathy. Don't you understand? The whole elaborate plot was staged so that she could worm her way into our confidence and into father's. She had already seen him in secret. I don't know *what* they are planning. I do know that she was taking some important part in it. The very fact that there was an attempt to murder her is proof enough that she *was* to win our sympathy, and—'

'Steady,' said Rollison. 'You're going too fast and getting illogical.'

'Isn't it obvious?' demanded Gwen.

It's far too complicated. I think they wanted to kill her and I think they were somehow prevented from doing so. And that is *not* only because I like the lady,' he added lightly and he gave her the impression that he was much happier, 'but I think I'm beginning to see the light. Tell me, did your mother ever see the so-called Countess?'

'Once,' said Gwen. 'We were out together and I pointed her out.'

'Was she alone?'

'No, she was with Pomeroy.'

'Did he see you?'

'I think so. We ignored him. We have never acknowledged him when it was avoidable.' She stubbed out the cigarette and lit another.

Rollison said: 'You and your mother saw her at the office or in the street and, apparently because you had seen her, probably because you pointed her out when she was with Pomeroy, Pomeroy and his friends want you dead. You are still in some danger, Gwen.'

'It—it doesn't make sense!'

'It makes more sense than some suggestions I've heard,' said Rollison. 'Now, listen to me. There is danger and there is only one way of avoiding it—by having the police in the house. You have a good excuse—the attempt to kill your mother.'

'We can't—'began Gwen.

'You must,' said Rollison. 'Surely you've the wit to see that the police will puzzle it out before they've finished. Even if it drags on for a few weeks until they catch Pomeroy. It will be far better to tell them yourself.'

She said: 'I can't do it.' She was distraught.

'Why not, Gwen?' he asked, gently.

'Because I am afraid for father!' Her voice rose. 'I don't know where he is but I think Pomeroy does; I think that he has been taken away so that they can do what they like with us! If you could find him, if you could be sure that he is in no danger I would tell the police everything but until then I can do nothing—*nothing*.'

'All right,' Rollison said. 'I'll find him for you. But you may not like it when it's done.'

'What do you mean?' she flashed.

'Haven't you always been afraid that he is a *willing* party to all that has happened?' asked Rollison and, as Gwen stared at him in utter dismay, he added: 'It's quite likely that he is, you know. Do you still want him found before the police are told anything?'

'Yes,' she said. 'But—I don't think you can find him.'

'I think I can find him in half an hour,' said Rollison. 'In fact in less—I can walk to the nursing home in twenty minutes.'

For a moment she looked as if she did not know what he meant. Then she backed away, staring at him with horror. She fumbled in a pocket in her skirt and Rollison watched her narrowly, not alarmed for himself but afraid for her. She took out a box of matches and toyed with it. At last she tossed it on to a table and put her hand into her pocket again. In her eyes was a wild look and although she was silent she was obviously beside herself.

'I shouldn't do that,' said Rollison.

He reached her in a stride and gripped her wrist. She had started to take her hand from her pocket and he saw the small automatic which she held. He pulled her arm up a little and then, twisting her wrist, he made her let go. The gun dropped. She began to struggle and he released her wrist and held her arms near the shoulders, tightly enough to hurt and to deny her any freedom of movement. Her face was distorted and her eyes were wild. He did not speak as he stared at her, trying to will her to give up the struggle.

Footsteps sounded in the hall, the front door opened and there came a murmur of voices.

CHAPTER SEVENTEEN

High Tension

ROLLISON COULD FEEL Gwendoline's body quivering. He relaxed his pressure slightly, seeing that her lips were also quivering and the wildness had faded from her eyes.

There was a tap at the door and, after a pause:

'Wait, please,' said Gwendoline, in an unsteady voice.

'It is Dr Renfrew, Miss Gwendoline,' said Farrow.

'Ask him to see my mother first,' she answered.

There was a pause but no sound of receding footsteps and then Renfrew spoke in an anxious voice.

'Are you all right, Gwen?'

'Give me just a few minutes,' Gwendoline said, 'I'll come upstairs then.'

'All right,' Renfrew sounded reluctant but the welcome noise of footsteps followed.

Gwendoline opened her lips but Rollison moved away from her towards the door. She turned and looked out of the window, standing quite still, the shaking fit still on her. Rollison reached the door without making a sound and then pulled it abruptly open.

Farrow backed away from the door, turning quickly on his heel. When he reached the door leading to the domestic quarters he looked round but averted his gaze when he saw Rollison staring after him. Rollison turned back into the room, closed the door and stepped to Gwendoline who took out a handkerchief and began to blow her nose.

'What can I say?' she said hoarsely.

'Say nothing,' said Rollison. He stooped down and picked up the gun and held it out to her.

She flinched. 'I don't want it!'

He put it into his pocket without a word but the fact that he had offered it to her would give her considerable psychological stimulus. He gave her a cigarette and they lit up.

'Thank God it was you,' she said.

He smiled. 'You see, I do sometimes turn up at the right moment!'

'I've behaved like a spiteful, venomous, murderous—'

'Wildcat,' Rollison completed for her. 'Daughter stirred to fury to save her father—it's a common attitude in reverse. And people do all manner of strange things when they're overwrought, as you've been overwrought during the past few weeks. Don't exaggerate it, Gwen, and don't think that I shall remember it against you! It must have been hard to keep going while believing that David was deliberately aiding and abetting crime.'

'It is *hellish*!' she said, her voice a-quiver.

'And it may be quite unjustified,' said Rollison. 'What made you think so badly of David?'

'Everything—points that way.'

'Everything being generally known or including something you haven't yet told me?'

'I've told you everything,' Gwendoline assured him. 'Rolly, please don't try to soften it for me. I know you think the same and I expect the police do. I've been trying to fool myself, trying to believe that it would not occur to anyone else but I know it's useless. I've wanted to believe the police are fools but I really know better.' She took a step towards him. 'Do they suspect him yet?'

'They haven't told me so,' said Rollison, 'but they've kept a lot to themselves and I can't blame them for that. You're wrong though, I don't suspect David—any more than I suspect anyone whose part I don't yet fully understand. My lost lady, for instance.'

'You're really taken by her, aren't you?' For the first time she spoke of the Lady of Lost Memory without bitterness.

If he were to gain her confidence, she must believe he was being wholly frank with her. So Rollison said: 'Yes, Gwen, I am.'

Her eyes softened, and she touched his arm.

'I hope you're right about her,' she conceded.

'Why have you been so set against her?'

'I've told you,' Gwen said, 'except—well, I suppose you'd better know this. One day when I went into David's room I found a letter which had slipped behind the bed. I shouldn't have read it, of course, but the first word was "Darling" and it wasn't in Hilda's handwriting. It was—a love letter. It was written without any restraint, it proved that they had known each other for a long time—for years, Rolly. That, with David!'

Rollison said, slowly: 'Was it signed?'

'Yes. Lila.'

'I see,' said Rollison.

In his mind's eye there was a picture of David Barrington-Ley, that wiry whippet of a man, good-looking in an attractive way. He was a man with whom many women might fall in love—and yet something rang false about the idea of the Lady of Lost Memory being in love with David, something rang as false about the idea of his being in love with her.

'It's quite true,' said Gwendoline, gently. 'I can show you the letter. I've kept it for several weeks. Would you like to see it?'

After a pause, Rollison said: 'Yes, of course, it may give more information. I'd like to keep it for a while. Was there an address?'

'It was headed New York and dated July.'

'She was there in July,' said Rollison. 'What made you connect Lila with the woman you saw at the office?'

'On the telephone, Pomeroy talked of her sometimes as Lila, and the Countess at others.'

'I see,' said Rollison, and then Gwen took the letter out of her handbag and handed it to him. It was deep blue paper, of good quality. He put it into his pocket with a word of thanks and tried to forget it but the tension which had possessed Gwendoline transferred itself to him. It was difficult to be dispassionate and detached, hard to think, to judge what questions to ask.

'Have you really told me every reason for suspecting David?' he asked at last.

'Yes,' she said, 'except the little indications, the trivial things one can't put into words. He has behaved strangely in some ways but in others he's been as he always is when he's got a big project in hand. He isn't exactly absent-minded but you can always tell that he's really thinking about something else—do you know what I mean?'

'I know,' said Rollison.

'He isn't a man to take kindly to blackmail,' said Gwendoline, 'and I came to the conclusion that either Pomeroy was blackmailing him or else everything was being done with his free consent. They're quite friendly, too—Pom and David to each other. David friendly with a little fat *louse* like that!'

'Does Hilda know?'

'She does *not!*' said Gwen, emphatically. 'That's been one of my fears, that she would find out. There isn't any need to tell her, is there?'

'None yet, at all events,' said Rollison. 'I'm not even sure that you're right.'

'I think you're just being kind. Do you really think he's at the nursing home?'

'Yes,' said Rollison. 'There isn't a better hiding-place, you know. Now you'd better see Dr Andrew or he'll come down and accuse me of dallying with your affections.' He smiled. 'Fond of Andrew?'

'Desperately.'

'Does he know what you suspect about David?'

'Yes—but no one else does.'

'I'd like a few words with him,' said Rollison.

'Of course,' said Gwendoline. 'I'll get him to come down.'

'I'd like to see him alone,' said Rollison, 'before he is told what I know. Do you mind?'

'All right,' said Gwendoline. She moved towards the door and when she drew level with him she paused and touched his arm. 'Rolly,' she said, 'I feel better than I have for weeks! It's hard to say thanks.'

'Don't even try,' said Rollison.

'I'm sorry about that letter,' she said, and then hurried out. There was more spring in her step.

Rollison sat down in an easy chair and lit a cigarette. The need in this case, as in so many others, was to disentangle the human emotions which played havoc with logic and often made black seem white. In the past he had not needed to worry about his own. Now he was defying logic and perhaps seeing black as white but even with the letter in his pocket he could not convince himself that he was wrong about the Lady of Lost Memory.

He was sitting with his eyes closed when Renfrew came in.

'Why, hallo,' Rollison greeted, jumping up at once. He smiled at the tall, lithe, dark doctor, who seemed a little anxious. 'How is Mrs Barrington-Ley?'

'She'll be all right,' said Renfrew.

'Gwen says she had a heart attack.'

'That's right.'

Rollison looked at him steadily, and although the other met his gaze, he seemed a little nervous. Obviously he expected the diagnosis to be challenged but Rollison tried another tack.

'Is photography a hobby of yours?' he asked, lightly.

'I do a bit,' said Renfrew.

'And do it well, I fancy,' said Rollison. 'When did you take the photograph of Lila, Countess Hollern? And why did you send me a print?'

Renfrew did not move and tried not to show dismay but he did not wholly succeed and Rollison smiled, glad now to have his thoughts running more freely, the problem gaining ascendancy in his mind.

'You did send it to me, didn't you?' he insisted.

'I don't know what you mean,' said Renfrew, in a strained voice.

'You do,' said Rollison. 'Look here, old chap, this business has gone far enough already. I think you sent the photograph to me because you knew that Gwen and Hilda were worried out of their minds. They had sworn you to secrecy but you were alarmed and wanted someone to look into it and you thought that the photograph would intrigue me.'

After a long pause, Renfrew tossed back his head, uttered a short laugh, and said:

'I didn't dream you'd guess!'

'Have I got it right?'

'Yes,' said Renfrew. 'Circumstances were hell for them, Hilda was as brittle as glass and Gwen was going to pieces. I knew that they were afraid—' He stopped abruptly, as if he realised that he had nearly made a damaging admission and, as he cast about in his mind for a plausible explanation, Rollison said:

'It's all right, Gwen's told me the whole story.'

'Everything!' exclaimed Renfrew.

'I think so. Her chief fear is that David is doing something he should not and that at all costs they wanted to avoid that becoming known.'

'It's right enough,' said Renfrew. He drew his hand across his forehead and dropped into a chair. 'It's an enormous relief to hear that you know, Rollison. I tried to persuade Gwen to tell you before but Pomeroy frightened her as well as Hilda. By George, it's been a nightmare! Can you'—he was suddenly eager—'can you see any light?'

'A few glims in the distance,' said Rollison, 'and I'm certainly not convinced that David is the villain of the piece. If he were being blackmailed, you know, he would do everything he could to prevent Hilda and Gwen from realising it. That's a point which you all missed, isn't it?'

'I suppose we did,' said Renfrew, slowly.

'Two things need immediate attention,' Rollison went on, briskly. 'First, what really happened to Hilda? Yes, Gwen confirmed what I had guessed, her heart-attack had unusual causes. You took risks, didn't you?'

'There wasn't any danger to her,' said Renfrew, defensively, 'and if we were right and David was behind the attack, well—what else *could* I do?'

'Not much,' said Rollison, 'What really happened?'

'Someone gave her a powerful injection of adrenaline,' said Renfrew. 'If she weren't as strong as a horse constitutionally, I mean—it would have been fatal but she threw off the effects. Gwen sent for me pretty quickly.'

'An injection,' murmured Rollison.

'She took a strong sleeping draught last night,' said Renfrew, 'anyone could have got into her room and pumped the stuff in without waking her. Rollison, I'm pretty sure that footman, Farrow, is up to no good.'

'Did you make up the sleeping draught?'

'Yes.'

'Who else knew about it?'

'Several people,' said Renfrew. 'Gwen, of course, Hilda's maid, the butler—I expect it was common gossip below stairs. There was nothing secret about the fact that there was trouble of some kind in the house and that Hilda wasn't sleeping well. I suppose the other thing you want settled,' went on Renfrew with an abrupt change of subject, 'is that photograph. That wasn't difficult—'

'It was taken before she arrived at the *Bal Masque*,' Rollison reminded him.

'Oh, yes, a week before. The woman dining with David at a small restaurant in the West End. I have a small Leica.'

'They saw you, of course?'

'Yes,' said Renfrew.

'Did David seem put out?'

'No—there was no cause for him to be, several other people were in the party. No one I know,' he added, 'I've tried to think where I've seen them before but I haven't succeeded.'

'How did you know they would be together?'

'I knew that David was going out to dinner and knew where,' said Renfrew. 'I'd been treating him for gastric trouble and there was no secret about that. I went with my sister. It was all quite usual. I didn't tell Gwen or Hilda, of course, I didn't want them worried unnecessarily. Er—and I'm afraid I sent a note to the Countess in your name,' he added, with a rather nervous laugh. 'I got a friend to meet her outside the nursing home and then sent her along to your flat. Er—no resentment, I hope.'

Rollison laughed. 'It was one of your good deeds.'

'Thanks,' said Renfrew. 'Well, what are you going to do now?'

Rollison told him that he was quite sure that the police should be in the house, to prevent further attacks on Gwendoline and Hilda. Renfrew raised no objection to the police being told about Hilda's collapse—there was no reason why he should not become suddenly suspicious of the cause of the heart attack.

The decision seemed to ease his mind. He could not stay much longer, he said, for he had several calls to make.

'Then telephone the Yard and make the report,' said Rollison, 'and tell them when you'll be free. I'll have a word with them afterwards.'

When Renfrew had finished speaking to an Inspector, Rollison took the telephone and suggested that a police-surgeon should be sent along at once to examine Mrs Barrington-Ley. He also asked that two men be stationed in the house. There was no demur.

'You're not taking many chances,' Renfrew said.

'We've taken too many already,' said Rollison.

'Yes, well, I must get off,' said Renfrew. 'Er—I can't thank you enough for the trouble you're taking and—and the way you're helping us.' He wrung Rollison's hand and hurried off.

Rollison was on edge to return to his flat or to the nursing home. Gwendoline did not come back and, after ten minutes, he went to the door. The hall was empty. The house was so large that Gwendoline was probably out of earshot. He waited for a few moments and then moved towards the stairs.

He had not taken three steps before he heard Gwendoline's voice, raised in alarm.

'Rolly! *Rolly!*'

He raced up the stairs, urged on by the urgency in her voice and she suddenly appeared on the landing, running towards him. She stopped to get her breath and waited for him, talking as he approached.

'Mother's door is locked, I can't get in, I saw Farrow come out of it; Rolly, what can we do?'

'Show me her room,' said Rollison.

She turned and hurried along the passages, turning now right and now left and then stopped outside a door which was too strong to be broken open by the pressure of a shoulder. Gwendoline banged on the door and called her step-mother's name while Rollison examined the lock closely. It was more suited to the door of a safe deposit than a bedroom.

'Is there another way in?' he demanded.

'No,' gasped Gwendoline, 'only the window. Father's room is next to hers but that's always locked.'

'Which is his?' asked Rollison.

She pointed towards the right and then called her stepmother's name again but there was no response. A maid came hurrying along, greatly alarmed, and up the stairs ran a white-haired man, the butler, followed by a younger man whom Rollison had not seen before.

Rollison pushed past the maid and reached the door on the left of Hilda's bedroom. It was ajar. He entered a small sitting-room, hurried across it, opened the window and looked out. It was a long drop to the ground but there were window-ledges and cornices on which he could stand and get a grip.

He climbed out as Gwendoline came in with the butler and the maid close behind her.

'Put a ladder beneath Hilda's window,' Rollison called.

He was clinging to the window sill with both hands, his head and shoulders above the level of the sill. He touched the top of the window below with his feet, let it take his weight and then measured the distance to the next window—one which looked too small for Hilda's room but might be a bathroom or dressing-room. There would be no great difficulty in getting to that, nor from it to the next room. He caught a glimpse of Renfrew behind Gwendoline, as he leaned sideways. He kept one hand on the sill—and, as he was groping for a hold on the next window ledge, he felt a sharp pain in the hand with which he was keeping his balance, a pain so sharp and so unexpected that he released his hold.

CHAPTER EIGHTEEN

Near Thing

ROLLISON TOPPLED BACKWARDS.

He had no grip with either hand but he was standing on the ledge below; but for that he would have fallen without a chance of recovery. He tried to sway forward and grasped at a ledge but it slipped from the tips of his fingers. By then he was almost upright and his feet were still on the ledge; so he leapt backwards, in the hope of falling on his feet.

There was a lawn with a stone path criss-crossing it immediately beneath him.

He hit the lawn with his heels and pitched backwards. The back of his head struck the lawn, not two inches from the path and the pain shot across his head, so violent that he gasped aloud. He felt a queer whirring sound in his head as his senses reeled. He was incapable of conscious effort but instinctively tried to sit up, only to fail and to collapse again.

Out of the dimness and the growing darkness, he heard a voice.

'Don't move, Guv'nor, don't move, yer ruddy fool!' A hand pressed his shoulder to the grass and then he was conscious of fingers touching his head. He felt no great pain. After a pause, the same voice came again. 'Well, nothing's broke, anyway.'

Someone else spoke. Rollison thought it was Gwendoline but he did not know for certain. He felt himself being lifted to a sitting position and there seemed to be nothing but voices and people crowding about him. He opened his eyes, and could see the people vaguely: two men in uniform, Gwendoline, the old butler and the younger man who was putting a ladder beneath a window. There were other men in plain clothes. It dawned on him that the police had arrived.

A stocky man bent over him and he heard a gruff voice say:

'You can't keep out of trouble, can you?'

It was Cray, the police-surgeon.

'Fell right on 'is 'ead, 'e did,' said the man who had first spoken and Rollison recognised the driver of his taxi.

'Head, eh?' said Cray. 'All right, Rollison, I won't hurt.' His fingers pressed Rollison's cranium. 'Now—feel anything?' Rollison shook his head and the pressure moved to another spot. 'Anything there? ... Or there? ... What about that?'

Rollison drew in his breath and forced himself to speak.

'I'm–all–right. Get into–Hilda's–room.'

'Hilda?' echoed Cray and looked up at one of the plainclothes men, an inspector from Scotland Yard.

'He means Mrs Barrington-Ley, sir,' said the butler, out of breath.

'*Get to her!*' gasped Rollison.

The Inspector and others turned and, as Rollison sat up, supported by the taxi driver who was on his knees behind him, he saw a policeman start to climb the ladder. A little comedy was enacted then when the Inspector pulled at the man's coat and told him to come down, then began to go up first.

'Take it easy, man,' said Cray, still standing in front of Rollison. 'They'll do what they can.'

'Help me up,' said Rollison.

'You'll be much better—' began Cray.

'Help me up!'

The taxi driver put his hands beneath Rollison's arm-pits and Cray took his forearms. Rollison was dizzy as he reached his feet and would have fallen but for their support. He stared towards the window where the Inspector was peering in. The uniformed policeman was half-way up the ladder, behind him.

Then the Inspector bent his elbow and cracked it against the glass. The report as the glass broke was like a pistol shot.

The man would not have done that unless faced with an emergency. Slowly, Rollison moved towards the house and the cabby and Cray went with him, one on either side.

'Must get upstairs,' Rollison muttered.

He thought the stairs would be too much for him and he had to rest three times on the way up but when he reached the landing he felt steadier. The butler had come behind them and now he went ahead and led the way towards Hilda's room. When they reached it the door was standing open and a police-constable was on duty outside. He stood aside for Rollison and Cray to enter but refused admittance to the cabby, who called out that he would wait outside.

Cray stepped swiftly to the bed on which Hilda lay.

It was a magnificent room, magnificently furnished, but Rollison had eyes only for Hilda who was on her back, her face a bluish grey, her eyes closed and her body motionless.

Rollison muttered:

'It's probably adrenaline, injected. I know she's had one dose.'

Cray opened his bag, took out his wallet and scribbled a few words on a card. He handed it to the policeman who had climbed the ladder and said:

'Get this made up at the nearest chemist and tell them it is urgent.'

'Right, sir.' The man hurried out and Cray began to examine Hilda, who did not stir. Rollison sat on the arm of a chair, staring at the bed; the Inspector stood on the far side. A few moments later, Gwendoline came in. She stifled a scream, moved slowly to Rollison's side and stood watching. Renfrew did not appear.

Only then was Rollison again aware of pain in his right hand. Looking down, he saw that there was a cut, still bleeding slightly, on the fleshy part of the wrist.

There was a big bump at the back of Rollison's head which was tender when he touched it and which prevented him from wearing a hat; apart from that, and a piece of lint and sticking plaster on his hand, he did not feel much ill-effect from his fall. He sat back in the easy chair by his desk with Jolly pouring out tea and the Lady of Lost Memory staring at him anxiously.

It was twenty-four hours since his fall. In the interim, he had been in no state to talk or think and his head still ached.

When he had left Barrington House, Dr Cray had said that there was a fair chance of Hilda recovering. She had been moved to hospital and Rollison was reasonably certain that she would be in no further danger. The footman, Farrow, had disappeared from Barrington House. Gwendoline and Renfrew had told their story to the police who had been non-committal but Rollison knew that a search was already being made for Farrow.

He had not yet heard Jolly's story, nor heard from Grice. The friendly cabby had brought him to the flat. Policemen remained at Barrington House with Gwendoline and Renfrew.

'Are you sure that you won't have a tot of whisky or brandy in the tea, sir?' asked Jolly.

'No thanks,' said Rollison. I'm all right.'

'All right!' exclaimed the Lady of Lost Memory. 'You look on the point of death!'

She was wearing a tweed suit which Jolly had obtained from a theatrical costumier's, was bare-headed and very lovely. It was not imagination that her eyes were filled with alarm. Rollison looked at her and sipped his tea before he spoke.

'I'm not quite as bad as that. You look delightful and much better.'

'Oh, please!' she said. 'Mr Rollison, what happened? Was it to do with me?'

'Only indirectly,' said Rollison. 'It's a long and complicated story and I don't feel up to telling it just now.'

'I think you should go back to bed,' she declared.

'I think I will turn in for an hour or two. You won't go out again, will you?'

'Not if you wish me to stay here.'

'I do.' Rollison stood up cautiously, went towards the door and then turned towards her. 'One small thing—Mrs Barrington-Ley is ill, I wonder if you would care to write a note of regret?'

'Of course,' she said. 'Is she seriously ill?'

'I think she will soon be all right,' said Rollison. 'Jolly will take the letter round.' He nodded and smiled, looking very woebegone and then entered the bedroom. Jolly closed the door and regarded Rollison with mild surprise.

'I don't want her to go out again and I can't shut her up in her own room,' said Rollison, 'so field headquarters are moved into here. What happened at the nursing home?'

'I saw Miss Armitage through the window, sir, but she was most adamant in her refusal to speak to me and consequently there was nothing I could do. The police were there very soon after me. Had the young woman been amenable I might have obtained useful information.'

'She was right enough,' said Rollison. 'I like to think that she's usually right. I hope Grice will soon turn up with the full story. You know what happened, I suppose?'

'I understand that the matron was murdered, sir.'

'Who told you that?'

'I waited until the Superintendent was there and then managed to overhear a little of what was said,' said Jolly.

'I see. Well, plenty was doing at Barrington House. I got off lightly. Are you in a receptive mood?'

'I think so, sir.'

'Good! Then listen to me. Take Farrow the footman first,' said Rollison. 'I have always thought him insolent but I am not sure whether that's the right word. He's not a footman and can't hide it. He might be employed by Pomeroy. But on the other hand, someone sent me that photograph and so was sure of impending trouble; the same person might have employed Farrow to work and watch at the house.'

'You mean, perhaps, Mr Barrington-Ley?' murmured Jolly.

'Yes.'

'Which would be a presumption of Mr Barrington-Ley's complete innocence.'

'I know,' said Rollison, 'that's what I want to presume. We'll have to check on Farrow. Now, what of Dr Renfrew?'

'I have made some further inquiries about him,' said Jolly. 'He is in some financial difficulties. I do not know in what degree but I hope to find out shortly.'

'If he's desperately hard up, he might do odd things for money,' said Rollison. 'Check that as soon as you can. And now...'

During the next quarter of an hour Rollison regaled Jolly with the salient points of the story while he undressed, put on pyjamas and a dressing-gown and got into bed gratefully. Jolly arranged the pillows so that he had support for his neck without pressure on the tender spot of his cranium. Then he stood by the side of the bed.

'And so,' said Rollison, at last, 'that's the whole story. What do you make of it?'

'I am rather at a loss, sir, to understand your uncertainty about the footman,' said Jolly. 'He certainly had every opportunity to inject the drug on two occasions—I assume that the second occasion was like the first, an injection of adrenaline?'

'It had the same effects and Cray thinks so.'

'Then it is reasonably certain that it was administered by the same person, sir.'

'Yes. Adrenaline isn't the easiest of drugs to obtain, you know.'

'No, sir, but unqualified persons have access to even more dangerous drugs than that—as you have often discovered.'

'The narcotics, yes. Adrenaline is a different matter. Why did Renfrew compromise his whole future by saying nothing about what he admits was an attempt at murder?'

'His explanation *appears* sufficient, sir,' said Jolly thoughtfully.

'Appears, yes. And it also would be a very good explanation if he actually gave the injection.' Rollison smiled at Jolly's expression. 'Suggestion not well received, Jolly?'

'Well, sir, with the utmost respect—would the man who first interested you in this matter and who arranged to send Madam here, take such a step?' asked Jolly.

'Meaning that the bump on my head is affecting my logic,' said Rollison. 'Many things which Renfrew has done seem unlikely. Why did he get a friend to take her to his home—I mean our guest— and then send her here in a taxi? And why did he keep her away from here for several hours?'

'Is it so remarkable, sir?'

'At the moment, I think so,' said Rollison. 'Renfrew was in a great hurry to get away after talking to me but he returned remarkably quickly. The last thing I saw when I was hanging from the window was Renfrew coming into the room. Then someone stabbed me in the hand with the unkind intention of making me break my neck.' When Jolly did not answer, Rollison went on: 'The doubts about the villainy of Farrow the footman come in there. He wasn't in that room. He had, apparently, fled the house before then. Renfrew was there with Miss Gwendoline, the butler, another footman and the maid. Any one of them could have come to the window and used the knife but it could not have been the footman.'

'I can follow you now, sir,' said Jolly obligingly. 'But Dr Renfrew—'

'Is practically engaged to Miss Gwendoline,' said Rollison. 'I would like to know a lot more about him. Background—real financial position, social reputation—all that kind of thing. Also, whether he possesses a Leica camera of the kind that can take excellent photographs through a waistcoat button-hole.'

'You mean that you doubt whether he *did* send the photograph?' said Jolly.

'I mean that I want to make sure,' said Rollison. 'I put that statement into his mouth and he accepted it after a noticeable pause. It might have been the result of being found out and being reluctant to admit it but at this stage why should he be reluctant? What is more,' went on Rollison, warming up, 'it might have been hesitation consequent upon getting an unexpected piece of information—hesitation while he made up his mind whether to turn it to his advantage or not. If Renfrew's mixed up in this he would be smart enough. If he didn't send me that photograph, he seized a unique opportunity to whitewash himself by agreeing that he did.'

'I suppose that is so, sir,' said Jolly, without enthusiasm.

'You still don't like it?' said Rollison.

Jolly spent a few moments in profound reflection and then said thoughtfully:

'I must admit that I see several difficulties, sir. For instance, would Miss Gwendoline be so easily deceived? You imply, sir, that Renfrew *and* Mr Barrington-Ley were working in concert—'

'Not Mr Barrington-Ley.'

'Then I don't quite understand you, sir.'

'It seems to me,' said Rollison, dreamily, 'that someone is most anxious that we should believe that David Barrington-Ley is a scoundrel. So much points to him. The police will, I've no doubt, soon be working on that assumption, but—I know him fairly well, Jolly.'

'If you will forgive me for saying so, sir, you rarely allow personal liking to affect your judgment.'

'Not liking only, Jolly—my knowledge of the man. Two things are possible. One, that he had been blackmailed by Pomeroy, Shayle and the others and forced to behave in this uncharacteristic manner. Two, that he is doing it willingly. His wife and daughter lean towards the second, presumably. I lean towards the first. If we assume that I'm wrong, we must also assume that Barrington-Ley has been a party to all that has happened. Many things, some apparently contradictory, have happened, Jolly. First—and I think the incident which brought it all out into the open and was not, therefore, premeditated—the arrival of the strange visitor to the *Bal Masque*. Afterwards, there came what appeared to be an attempt to murder her but because of what we have heard of Marcus Shayle's instructions to Phyllis Armitage, that might have been simply an attempt to frighten her and encourage her to talk more freely. A nurse is a likely confidante, isn't she?'

'Yes, sir, I think that is reasonable.'

'There followed what I think was an attempt on Phyllis Armitage's life which I was able to stop before it got really under way. Then a series of minor incidents followed with the sudden rush of events in the last few days. Barrington-Ley's disappearance—the attempt to murder Miss Gwendoline, the two attempts on Mrs Barrington-Ley's life and, let's face it, the attempt to-day on mine. Would a man attempt to murder his own daughter—or give instructions for such an attempt to be carried out and would he kill his own wife?'

After a pause, Jolly said:

'According to the letter which Miss Gwendoline gave you, sir, there is a motive for his wishing his wife dead.'

'Ah, yes,' said Rollison. 'But why his daughter?'

'She might suspect the truth, sir. From what you have told me, it is very likely that she had kept that back. It would be natural if she held back some of her grounds for suspicion of her father's activities, if they included the attempt to murder Mrs Barrington-Ley.'

'Yes,' said Rollison, slowly. 'Yes. But I don't believe it! Jolly, see if Lady Lost has written the letter to Mrs Barrington-Ley yet and, if she has, let me see it before you deliver it.'

'Very good, sir,' said Jolly.

While he was gone, Rollison took the love-letter from his wallet and, for the first time, read it through. He did not enjoy it. The letter was well-written but the English was a little stilted. It talked of difficulties, of the fact that "you" have not your freedom of love and longing—and when he finished, Rollison closed his eyes for a few moments and wished that the Lady of Lost Memory had never come within his ken.

Then Jolly came in, carrying a letter.

The writing of the letter which Gwendoline had found was bold and clear; at a glance, the writing on the envelope which had just been addressed looked equally bold and clear. After a close inspection, he had to acknowledge that the two letters were written by the same person.

He said: 'What is Lady Lost doing, Jolly?'

'She is in her room with the maid, sir.'

'I see. Jolly—what do you make of it now? Don't hold your fire, let me know how you see the whole thing.'

Jolly said slowly: 'There are some points which still mystify me, sir, but on others I think I am fairly clear. Unlike you, sir I incline towards the theory that Mr Barrington-Ley is a willing party to the crimes, that he wishes to be free to marry Lady Lost, that to get his way he would even murder his daughter. For the rest, sir, it appears to me that he may be in some financial difficulties and that he is tiding over the period by using the money which Lady Lost raised in America for the Yugoslav Relief Fund.' Jolly paused and then asked quietly: 'Shall I go on, sir?'

'Yes,' said Rollison.

'If I am right, then most of the other things fall into perspective,' said Jolly. 'The one which might appear puzzling is the attack on you but remember, sir, that members of the staff at Barrington House have, undoubtedly, a staunch loyalty to their master. The butler or even the maid, realising that you constituted a great danger, might have made you fall, sir.'

'And then?' asked Rollison.

'Isn't that sufficient?' asked Jolly.

'No,' said Rollison, emphatically. 'It's nothing like enough. You put David Barrington-Ley and—we'd better use this title now—the Countess together as a brace of unscrupulous scoundrels to whom murder and fraud are as meat and drink. And you fail to explain two things—first, that there was the attempt on the Countess—'

'Which you have admitted was a fake attempt, sir.'

'I admitted that it might be. All right, there's a second thing, Jolly. If they are what you think they are, if they have conspired to do these things, why did the Countess arrive, uninvited and unexpected, at that party? And was she at Malloy's?'

Jolly murmured: 'That first *is* mystifying, sir, but it may have been a way in which the Countess was to be introduced to the family and invited to stay for a while at Barrington House. We know that such an invitation was almost a foregone conclusion. If Mr Barrington-Ley worked on his knowledge of his wife's likely reaction, there is nothing surprising in that. And she might have been deliberately hiding at Malloy's.'

'All right—what about the murder of the Matron?'

'If you are right and Mr Barrington-Ley has been in hiding there the Matron, who is a friend of the family, might have threatened to tell the police. That would provide motive enough, sir.'

'Yes,' said Rollison, after a pause. 'I suppose it would.' He looked at Jolly with his head on one side. 'In fact you're right, you have a plausible case, you have worked this up as brilliantly as if you were a policeman! Do you know what I think about it?'

'No, sir,' said Jolly.

'I think it's poppycock!'

'I *beg* your pardon, sir?'

'Poppycock! Balderdash! Our friend the farrago of nonsense—oh, reasonable, logical, carefully prepared nonsense but nonsense none the less. And what is more,' said Rollison, leaning forward and pointing a finger at his man, 'I know what you are thinking and I know what Grice will say—I am influenced first by my liking for David Barrington-Ley and secondly by my quite incomprehensible confidence in Lady Lost. All right, Jolly! A lovely face and a lady in distress have blinded me to the facts—all right! I'm blind. But before you take me for treatment, find out what you can about Renfrew. Bring me the information as quickly as you can. Then find out what you can about Janice Armitage—not her sister but Janice, the young one. The police will be watching her and probably making inquiries but you might make a lucky strike.'

'I am ready to go at once, sir.

When Jolly had gone out of the room, less disapproving than dismayed, Rollison scowled at the ceiling. He heard Jolly walk across the hall and then the "maid" spoke. Almost at the same moment the front door bell rang. There was murmur of voices and Rollison recognised Grice's. Jolly opened the door again and Grice came in, smiling as if all was right with the world. Yet beneath that smile there was a hint of uneasiness, as if he knew that he had come on an unpleasant errand.

'I told you so,' moaned Rollison. 'He has it all sewn up, cadavers and all. All right, Jolly, you get busy. Remember that our reputation depends on this.' He waited until the door was closed and then stared into Grice's smiling face. Deliberately, he said, 'Whatever you think, it's wrong.'

'Well,' said Grice, 'I've got Barrington-Ley under arrest. He was at the nursing home, masquerading as a patient.'

CHAPTER NINETEEN

Renfrew

'MY DEAR CHAP,' said Rollison, 'I told Jolly an hour ago that you'd find him there and I told Gwendoline three hours before where you'd find him if you thought of looking. Now supposing you stop grinning like a sleek and over-fed Cheshire cat and examine your case for its flaws.'

Grice laughed. 'You must have had a nasty bump!'

'I even had a fall,' said Rollison. 'Let me remind you that no fall is so long or heavy as that which comes after pride and never was pride so arrogant as yours just now. You think you've got it all solved, don't you?'

'Yes,' said Grice, and he was no longer smiling. 'Rolly, what do you really think of the Countess?'

'I thought you knew,' said Rollison.

Grice said: 'I've been thinking that it would be like you to pretend to have fallen for her, simply to pull the wool over my eyes.'

'Not at all true,' said Rollison. 'Any wool blinding you was pulled by your own fair hand.' He was trying not to let himself feel so acutely depressed, trying to appear lightly sarcastic and so prepare himself for what Grice had to say. 'Has Barrington-Ley talked?'

'No, except to say that he was drugged and woke up to find himself at the nursing home.'

'And you don't believe him?'

'I do not,' said Grice.

'All right, let it come,' said Rollison.

Grice said, slowly: 'We've also caught Pomeroy.'

'Remarkable! But isn't catching crooks all part of police service?'

'And Shayle and Malloy,' said Grice.

'Quite a birthday for the police!' said Rollison.

'I wish you wouldn't behave like this,' said Grice. 'You can't always be right, you know. The truth is—'

'The truth is that you think you've come to the end,' said Rollison, 'and this is how you've worked it out.' He did not give Grice a chance to interrupt but talked swiftly. He put the case which Jolly had outlined but in fewer words and with more telling effect and he could see that Grice, if not actually astonished, grew more surprised as each item in the indictment against Barrington-Ley and the Countess unfolded.

Rollison spared himself nothing and even mentioned the love-letter which Gwendoline had found.

When he had finished, Grice said:

'If you were advancing your own opinions and not guessing mine, I would still call it miraculous!'

'They're Jolly's opinions,' said Rollison. 'Have you got anything to support such a case?'

'Yes,' said Grice. 'Jolly was always more stable than you.'

'Never mind Jolly—let's have your case,' said Rollison.

One half of his mind was paying close attention to what Grice said; the other was busy with thoughts of Lila, Countess Hollern. He thought she knew that he had not wanted to talk in front of her and was therefore staying in her room. It was painful to think of her and it grew more painful as Grice went on.

'Both firms of Pomeroy, Ward & Pomeroy are deeply involved,' said Grice. 'Your Pomeroy is actually a partner of the accountants, although the others once denied any knowledge of him. The firm is handling the accounts of the Relief Fund, as I've said, *and into the firm's account all the American money was paid.*'

'Ah,' said Rollison.

'Early this year,' Grice continued, 'Barrington-Ley suddenly changed his accountants. He had employed the same firm for many years but he transferred to Pomeroy, Ward & Pomeroy. On the firm's statement, the accounts are in very bad order. Fat Pomeroy agrees and says that Barrington-Ley knew it. His purpose was to get Pomeroy's to produce accounts which would appear satisfactory. The Relief Fund money was to help to stabilise the position.'

'Wholesale falsification of accounts,' murmured Rollison.

'Yes. There can't be any reasonable doubt about it.'

'Fat Pomeroy denied any share in the firm and the firm denied him.'

'That isn't a crime in itself,' said Grice. 'He told me that until the last moment he hoped Barrington-Ley would be able to put his affairs in order. He—fat Pomeroy—became involved and decided to try to cover up the shortages. The rest followed naturally.'

'It could be the answer,' Rollison said. 'Have you seen the accounts?'

'Not yet but we're applying for a Court Order to see them as well as the various banking accounts.'

'So you're relying on fat Pomeroy's word.'

'Why on earth should he lie at this juncture?' demanded Grice. 'Shayle supports him in every statement and their statements were made independently. Malloy knows little about it, apparently he was employed to supply violence when necessary. He employed the painter at Miss Armitage's flat—yes, you were right about that, they wanted her dead. They don't admit intent to murder, of course, only to frighten.'

'Why frighten?'

'They thought Janice Armitage had told her sister where to find Marcus Shayle and in any case she could incriminate Shayle—as she did. Once we knew her story, the rest came logically. They were right to want her out of the way if they were to save themselves.'

'Yes,' said Rollison. 'But there's an answer to your earlier question— why should Pomeroy and Shayle lie at this juncture? Neither lies nor the truth will save them from punishment but a confession, talk of King's Evidence, putting the principal blame on Barrington-Ley—all those will help them.'

'Nonsense! They've practically admitted complicity in murder!'

'Oh, my dear chap,' said Rollison. 'There was no murder until the matron's. Has Malloy talked?'

'No.'

'But they've admitted they used him to provide the strong-arm men, you say. They'll doubtless insist that he was instructed not to commit murder—'

'They won't get away with that,' interrupted Grice. 'They've gone too far in their admissions.'

'Don't forget that unless they killed the matron, which doesn't seem likely, there's no murder charge against them,' said Rollison. 'They're safe enough on that. They're putting the blame on to Barrington-Ley, standing together to negate his evidence. Now you've got them, it's their only wise course. But never mind, you've got your case, short of the matron's murder. Let's leave the sore subject of who killed her. When will you be able to examine the accounts?'

'This evening, I expect.'

'You can falsify accounts two ways,' said Rollison. 'You can make good ones seem bad, as well as bad ones seem good. Don't forget that.'

'I've never known you quite like this,' said Grice. 'It isn't any use trying to deny the facts.'

'I question their accuracy,' Rollison said. 'There are two people in whom I believe—the Countess and Barrington-Ley. They are not, in my view, people who would become involved in such an affair as this of their own free will. That's the issue, and your answer is different from mine.'

'Very different, apparently,' said Grice.

Rollison said: 'And now you want to arrest the Countess for conspiring with Barrington-Ley, I suppose?'

'I must take her along with me,' said Grice, evasively.

'On a charge of conspiring to defraud?'

'I haven't got as far as that yet.'

'I'm glad that you're wide awake enough for that,' said Rollison, sitting up and pushing the eiderdown back. 'You certainly haven't got as far, you haven't a charge of any kind which you can prefer against her. Pretending to having lost her memory? You might construe it into being a public nuisance but if I were you I wouldn't try. Poisoning herself? Even you don't believe she tried to commit suicide. And everything else that has happened in England in this affair took place when she was at the nursing home with a sound alibi, an alibi your own men provided, or else here with one that the maid, Jolly, or I can provide. On the evidence of one letter and some gossip you can assume that she was having an affair with Barrington-Ley but that's no crime. Oh, take her along with you, old chap! Go through the motions of charge and arrest and I'll be on the doorstep with a complaint of wrongful detention before you can say knife.'

'Now, Rolly—'

'Now Rolly be damned!' said Rollison. 'Where are my trousers?'

He took them from a chair. 'I've warned you.' He sat down and pulled on his trousers, staring at Grice all the time. 'Wrongful detention after you've been warned is serious. You haven't a case, you know as well as I do that if you take her up before the magistrate you'll get sharp words from the gentleman unless you've a lot more to go on than you've told me.'

Grice's expression told him that he had not.

'And there is another thing,' said Rollison, vehemently. 'The police are no fools but sometimes they have been fooled. You are being properly and completely diddled. On the evidence of a well-known East End crook who hires out strong men for any beastly job that offers, of Pomeroy, a renegade solicitor-cum-accountant and Marcus Shayle, himself detained on a charge of attempted murder, you're assuming that Barrington-Ley is guilty of all manner of heinous crimes. Why? Only because it fits your own theory.'

'He hasn't said a word in his own defence.'

'I should think not! David's a good fellow, he would give you a chance of apologising nicely and withdrawing the charge before he started to point out how completely you've been fooled. Where's my coat?' He finished tying his tie, put on his coat and went on talking rapidly. 'I'm serious. Unless you're keeping something back or are taking steps to extradite the Countess, you'll arrest or detain her at your own risk and against all the opposition I can rake up—be it fair or foul!'

Grice said: 'If I'd wanted further evidence against Barrington-Ley, I would have it in your story of the love-letter written to him by the Countess.' He was deliberately brutal.

'Bah.'

'Did you or did you not tell me about that letter?'

'I did. Here, I'll show it to you.' Rollison tossed the letter to Grice and waited while he read it through and there was a curious expression in his eyes as he watched. He seemed almost elated.

Grice handed it back, but said:

'I shall probably need that as evidence.'

'That's fine,' said Rollison, refusing to take it. 'Use it as evidence! Try to get any conviction of any kind on the strength of it. Why, you addlepate, David Barrington-Ley's name *isn't even mentioned*! It was in his possession, or rather found behind his dressing-table, but there isn't any evidence at all he received it or read it. Why shouldn't my lady write to her beloved? I tell you that if you arrest or detain her, I'll move heaven and earth to prove you a complete fool.'

'I shall leave the maid with her,' Grice said, after a long pause, 'and I shall have her closely followed if she leaves this flat.'

Rollison raised his hands and beamed. He was almost gay, something had put new life into him.

'Threat withdrawn?'

'You know perfectly well that I can't take her with me if you're going to act like that,' said Grice. 'I don't think much of it, Rolly. You're taking advantage of the fact that I told you what I was going to do.'

Rollison said: 'Now be reasonable! I gave you good warning. I don't want you to make a fool of yourself and the police force and when this affair really breaks you'll agree that it was a good thing. Er—seriously, now.'

'Well?' said Grice.

'What happened at the nursing home?'

Grice said, grudgingly. 'Phyllis Armitage went to see the matron, at the matron's request, and she found the matron dead.'

'By poisoning?'

'Yes.'

'Is Phyllis under suspicion?'

'No. The poison must have been taken an hour before she arrived. Barrington-Ley is under suspicion. He was there.'

'Poor David!' said Rollison. 'Well, old chap, I don't want you to feel that you're not welcome but I've a call to make. Stay here if you like, of course, I'll trust you not to worry the Countess.'

'Where are you going?' demanded Grice.

'To see Phyllis Armitage?'

'Why?'

'Because I think they may have wanted to kill her for more reasons than one,' said Rollison, 'and because she may know why, without realising it.'

'I hope you don't make a mistake,' Grice said. He followed Rollison out of the room and they went to the front door. Before

Rollison opened it, Grice turned and said with unusual seriousness: 'Rolly, did you know the Countess before this started?'

'Great Scott, no!'

'Are you sure?' demanded Grice.

'I am quite sure,' said Rollison. 'What makes you doubt it? I had her photograph but I've told you about that.'

'I don't mean her photograph,' said Grice. 'I can't believe that a woman whom you've known for such a short time would affect you like this.'

Rollison said: 'Odd, isn't it? I can hardly believe it myself! And that reminds me, I must tell her that I'm going out.'

He felt not only less on edge but possessed by an almost feverish excitement. Nothing seemed quite normal except the smile with which the Lady of Lost Memory greeted him when he opened the door. She was sitting by the window, reading; the "maid" was opposite her, sewing.

'Are you better, so soon?' she asked.

'I was never really ill,' said Rollison. 'Don't get up.' He stepped across the room as she stood up and shifted her chair. 'But don't sit so that you can be seen from the street,' he said. 'And remember this—if anyone, *any*one asks you questions, even your maid, don't answer. Don't answer any kind of question put to you by anyone except me.'

'If you insist upon it, I will not,' she said but she was puzzled and no longer smiling. 'What troubles you, Mr Rollison?'

'Unpleasant people,' said Rollison.

Downstairs, actually in the hall of the building, one of Grice's men saluted him. In the street were two other men and to one of them Grice, leaning out of his car, was talking earnestly. Rollison went the other way, soon found a taxi and within twenty minutes he was walking up the stairs leading to Phyllis Armitage's flatlet. The painters had finished and the new paint was already scratched in places.

Phyllis herself answered his knock. She did not look particularly surprised but asked him in.

'I suppose you've seen the police,' she said.

'Yes, and we're not friends,' said Rollison. 'Miss Armitage, I haven't much time and I must have the answer to a single question before I go.'

'If I know the answer, I'll tell you,' she promised.

'Think back to the afternoon when you left the nursing home.'

She frowned. 'Yes.'

'The matron had tea with the patient and the poison was administered before tea—that's right, isn't it?'

'Yes, so I was told.'

'You left the room about half-past three.'

'It was a little earlier.'

'Who came into the room before you left? I don't mean Marcus Shayle, I mean who else on the staff or connected with the nursing home.'

'No one,' said Phyllis, eyeing him steadily.

'Are you quite sure?' demanded Rollison. 'I mean, someone who had every right to be there, whose presence you would not perhaps notice specially, who always came about that time, who—' He broke off and there was a glint in his eyes. 'Ah, you've remembered! Who was it?'

She said slowly: 'Dr Renfrew came in.'

'Did he send you out at all?'

'I had to take a message to the matron, yes.'

'So Renfrew was with her alone,' said Rollison and there was a great relief in his mind. 'That's splendid! You're prepared to swear to it?'

'Of course. He came every afternoon about that time, I didn't really notice it. I am quite sure there was no one else.'

'That's fine,' declared Rollison. 'I think I'll call that a day. Will you write that statement down and sign it?'

'Of course,' she said, now really puzzled, 'but what has Dr Renfrew to do with it?'

'More than we realise yet,' said Rollison.

He watched her as she wrote swiftly, signed what she had written, blotted it and handed it to him. He tucked the statement into his wallet and turned to go. She followed him and said in a low-pitched voice:

'Mr Rollison, is my sister in serious trouble?'

'I don't think so,' said Rollison. 'Why?'

'If the police thought she deliberately refused to tell them where

Marcus Shayle could be found, they might—well, they might do anything.'

'They won't do anything about that,' said Rollison.

He smiled reassuringly and hurried out; and outside was one of
Grice's men.

Rollison stopped by his side and said: 'Be very careful of Miss
Armitage. If anyone goes to the house, follow close on their heels.'

'I have my instructions, sir,' said the man.

'Are they the same as mine have been?'

'Pretty nearly.'

Rollison had kept his taxi waiting and returned to Gresham Terrace
where he left it waiting again and hurried upstairs. He was not
surprised when the door was opened by Jolly before he reached it, nor
that Jolly looked as if he had great news.

'Shall we go into your bedroom, sir?' asked Jolly, in a whisper.

'All right,' said Rollison and, once they were there, asked eagerly:
'Well, Jolly?'

'I thought it better to return before I made inquiries about Miss
Janice Armitage, sir.'

'What news about Renfrew?'

'He is *very* heavily in debt, sir.'

'Splendid! How did you find out?'

'From his receptionist. It is apparently an open secret to trades-
people and the like—I called prepared to ask indirect questions,
and—ahem—I was taken for a bailiff, sir.'

'It can't be as bad as that!'

'It is very bad, I assure you—the receptionist, a rather garrulous
lady of middle age, has not been paid her salary for over three
months. What is more, sir, much of the equipment at the surgery is
not paid for, the receptionist told me that several of the firms who
supplied it have threatened to take it back unless payment is made.
Apparently Dr Renfrew has lived on a very expensive scale.'

'The simple things!' exclaimed Rollison. 'It couldn't be better.
Did you get anything else?'

'One or two other things, sir. The receptionist was quite an intelligent
woman and she was quick to recognise the description which I drew for
her—of Pomeroy.'

'Is he a frequent visitor?' demanded Rollison.

'Less frequent than a few months ago,' said Jolly. 'And the other thing is perhaps the most significant of them all. The receptionist, with whom I got on very well indeed, confided that she knows that everything stands or falls—I use her own expression, sir—by his relationship with the Barrington-Ley family. The strong impression which the receptionist has is that he hopes to marry Miss Gwendoline and so solve his financial difficulties.'

'Yes,' said Rollison. 'Yes, he would.'

'I hope it helps a little, sir.'

'It helps a lot, for Renfrew probably poisoned Lady Lost. Stay here, Jolly. The police are watching the flat, as you've doubtless noticed, but I don't want to take any chances with her.'

'I will be at hand for any emergency,' said Jolly. 'Are you likely to be long, sir?'

'I hope not,' said Rollison. 'I'm going to see Renfrew.'

'May I inform Mr Grice, if he should inquire?'

'Provided I've first had half an hour with Renfrew on my own,' said Rollison.

He left as hurriedly as he had arrived and gave the taxi driver Renfrew's Wimpole Street address. Renfrew had been left out of Grice's calculations but that was a mistake. There had been other mistakes, not least his own, but he believed he had come to the end of them now.

The middle-aged receptionist, a neat, prim woman, opened the door and when Rollison said that he had no appointment, said that she was afraid that Dr Renfrew would not be able to see him. He was with one patient, another was waiting and he had urgent calls to make after that. The woman looked fretful, as if she were very disillusioned of the young and handsome Dr Renfrew.

'Take him my card,' said Rollison.

'I will give it to him when he finishes his present appointment,' said the woman. 'But I think for a moment that it will be of any use your waiting. He is *very* busy today.'

'All the same, I'll wait,' said Rollison.

She shrugged her shoulders resignedly and then opened the door of the waiting-room. It was a long, impressive room with a cold atmosphere perhaps suggested by the highly-polished Sheraton furniture. A long narrow dining-table held a dozen shiny magazines, dining chairs were pushed beneath the table and chairs with wooden arms were dotted about the sides. The sun shone through the fine net curtains at the windows and on the head of a man who suddenly hid his face behind a magazine as Rollison entered.

The receptionist went out, closing the door with a decided snap.

Rollison picked up a magazine without sending more than a cursory glance at the other "patient" but the quick movement had caught his eye. He glanced over the top of a *Sphere* and the other looked furtively over *Punch*. When he realised that Rollison was staring at him, he averted his eyes and tried to hide his face again but he was too late and Rollison recognised Farrow the footman.

Slowly, and without speaking, both men stood up.

CHAPTER TWENTY

Motives

THEY STOOD QUITE still, staring at each other. Rollison expected Farrow to show some sign of fear but, now that he had been recognised, the footman seemed prepared to put a bold face on it.

Rollison said: 'I suppose you know that you are wanted for the murder of Mrs Barrington-Ley.'

The footman said, sharply: 'Is she dead?'

'There isn't much hope for her,' said Rollison. 'You know what happened, don't you?'

'What?' Farrow did not seem unduly alarmed.

'She was given two injections of adrenaline, which affects the heart, and you had the opportunity each time. There is a warrant out for your arrest.'

'*I* didn't do it,' said Farrow. There was no bluster about him, only a quiet and impressive confidence. 'I think I know who did, though.'

'So do I,' said Rollison and, moving towards the other, went on very quietly: 'Why have you come to see Renfrew?'

'Why have *you*?'

'I don't think we're going to get much further if we keep talking at cross purposes,' said Rollison. He felt a quickening sense of urgency and he glanced over his shoulder, half afraid that Renfrew might come in. 'I don't think you gave her the injections but appearances are against you and you are a sitting bird. If you know anything about this business, you probably know that already several people have been cleverly framed and blamed for crimes they did not commit. Barrington-Ley is among them and might still pay for another man's crimes. If you can give him the slightest help, you'll also help yourself.'

'I wonder,' said Farrow.

'You haven't much time to decide,' Rollison said. 'Why did you go to work at Barrington House?'

'Because I was paid for it,' said Farrow. He gave a quick, mirthless smile. 'I didn't know what I was letting myself in for!'

'From which inquiry agency did Mrs Barrington-Ley hire you?'

For the first time he really surprised the man who moved back a pace and stumbled against a chair. For a shot in the dark it was an achievement and with its success many other things fell into their right perspective. Rollison hardly heard Farrow's astonished: 'Well, I'm damned!' but realised for the first time something of the depth of Hilda's mental torment. She had suspected David of wanting to be rid of her, suspected him also of fraud and to try to find out the truth *she had employed a man from a private detective agency.* Pomeroy had raised no objection, had probably give his outward support for such a man as Farrow was a ready-made victim for the frame-up which was planned.

'I didn't think anyone would spot it,' Farrow said, in a wondering tone. 'I'm from Morgan's Bureau. I've heard of you, but—'

'Let's cut out everything that's irrelevant,' urged Rollison. 'Renfrew may come in at any moment and we want to get this ironed out quickly. Mrs Barrington-Ley employed you to watch her husband, did she?'

'Yes.'

'For what reasons?'

'She was pretty vague. She said she thought he was worried and being blackmailed but I soon found out she was afraid he was having an *affaire* and planning to murder her,' said Farrow. He joined Rollison and spoke in a low-pitched voice, glancing at the door from time to time. 'I haven't found a thing against Barrington-Ley. Absolutely nothing at all. The little fat swab, Pomeroy, has fooled B-L, I know that, but I don't know what he's after. I do know that *Renfrew* tried to do away with Mrs B-L. I went into her room soon after he'd come out, after the first attack, and if I hadn't made it plain that I had suspected him, I think she would have died. He pulled her round and I let him think that I would keep my mouth shut for a share of the spoils. I'm here to collect information, not spoils! I've made a full report in writing to the office, I'm not putting anything across you. I've come across a lot of people in my time but I've never met a woman with more guts than Mrs B-L. That's the truth, Mr Rollison, and if I can put this clever doctor on the spot, that's where he's going.'

'He's on it,' said Rollison.

Farrow snapped: 'Are you sure?'

'Yes, quite sure. Have you got anything else?'

'Renfrew's up to his neck in debt,' said Farrow. 'He thinks he can put himself right by marrying Gwendoline. She's lent him a small fortune already but he just can't hold money, his fingers are greased. His only hope is to get a bumper marriage settlement and he'll get a better one if Mrs B-L is dead. The daughter will inherit all there is, then, and Renfrew will be on a good thing.' Farrow scowled. 'I *think* he's going to have a cut at polishing off Barrington-Ley when Mrs B-L is dead and buried but I can't be sure of that. What are *your* ideas?'

'Not far removed from yours,' said Rollison, softly. 'I didn't see that motive but I certainly should have done. Do you know anything about Pomeroy and the Yugoslav Relief Fund?'

'Not much,' said Farrow. 'Pomeroy's as slippery as they come. All I know is that he's an outsize crook and Barrington-Ley has been taken in by him—*and* I don't mean maybe! Does that Fund matter?'

'Yes,' said Rollison. 'And I think I see where it comes in. I—'

He broke off for Farrow, looking at the door, suddenly backed away and sat down. But it was only the receptionist, who looked even more sour.

'Dr Renfrew will see Mr Farrow,' she said, with a sharp glance at Rollison, 'and you *after*wards. He says he may be some time.

'I think we'll see him together,' said Rollison. He took the receptionist's arm and she resisted in a flurry of alarm. 'We're on police business.'

'Police!' she gasped.

She stared at them, white-faced, as they crossed the hall to a room marked *Dr Renfrew—Surgery*. But she made no effort to interfere and Rollison, with a detaining hand on Farrow's arm, waited until she had disappeared through another door. Then he said softly:

'Go in and leave the door ajar, will you?'

'Any special questions?' asked Farrow.

'No, but speak clearly.'

Farrow was as helpful now as he had been hostile before and he managed to leave the door unlatched without it being noticed so that Rollison could hear every word that was said. He realised that someone else was in the room besides Renfrew but did not yet know who it was.

Renfrew said: 'I told you to come tomorrow, Farrow.'

'It wasn't soon enough,' said Farrow, 'I'm taking enough chances as it is.' He played up well, adding nervously: 'How do I know *I* won't be arrested for that murder?'

'She's not dead yet,' said Renfrew, damning himself utterly. 'I'll see that you're all right, Farrow, but not now. Did you see Rollison in the waiting-room?'

'Yes.'

'Did he speak?'

'No, but I don't like the way he looks at me.'

'You fool!' came a woman's voice with a note of searing contempt which probably made Farrow flinch. 'You don't like the way he *looks* at you! Why—'

'Be quiet, Gwen,' said Renfrew, nervously.

Rollison, standing quite still, was aghast at the truth which was now all too evident. *Gwendoline* was in that room. She was a party to all that Renfrew had done, was in his full confidence and intent on keeping Farrow quiet.

So many puzzles were solved with that realisation. Gwen's manner before the attack on her; she was afraid he suspected the truth and in a mad moment, had thought of killing him. Her lies about seeing the Lady of Lost Memory, her hatred—to provide grounds for her behaviour—her anxiety to keep the affair from the police, her complaisance with Pomeroy who was a party to the plot; all those things fell into place. There were others.

Everything Gwen and Renfrew had told him could be discounted. He should have realised before then Gwen had cut his hand to try to send him to his death. Renfrew had not been near enough to the window to use a knife. Her professed anxiety for her father and her carefully prepared story of her suspicions of him—all was false. She had once called at the Strand office of Pomeroy, Ward & Pomeroy but he had not paid that enough attention.

How she had lied!

All that passed through Rollison's mind as he stood in the hall. Then he pushed the door open slowly and could sense the sudden tension which had sprung into the room but he could not hurry; in whatever else he had been right, he had completely misjudged Gwendoline.

He went in.

Renfrew was sitting at a bureau desk in a large, plainly furnished surgery and Gwendoline was by his side. When she saw Rollison she jumped to her feet and into her eyes sprang an expression which he had seen before, at the time when she had drawn an automatic from her pocket. Then he had thought her overwrought and hardly responsible for her actions but now fear made her desperate.

Renfrew backed further away. Gwendoline snatched her bag from the table and opened it.

Rollison said: 'I shouldn't do that.' The words were the same as he had used before, only their tone was different. She kept her hand inside her bag and glared at him while Renfrew, making a desperate effort to regain his self-control, stepped forward and slammed the door, avoiding Farrow who tried to stop him.

'It's all right,' said Rollison to Farrow. He was still looking at Gwendoline and she returned his stare with all the malignance of which she was capable, cold, murderous, utterly evil. 'So this is how it is! With Hilda dead you would be worth a fortune on your father's death.'

She said: 'Don't move an inch.'

He stood quite still.

'And I thought Renfrew was the evil genius! I almost wish that Hilda would die; you would then be hanged, the pair of you—hanged by the neck until you are dead—'

'*Be quiet!*' screamed Gwendoline.

'With a bandage over your eyes and only the hangman on the gallows with you,' said Rollison, in a voice low-pitched with cold fury. 'Clever Gwendoline! You showed Hilda that letter you found, didn't you? You made her suspicious of David, you tortured her mentally and you tortured him, setting one against the other while you stood by and gloated, seeing your plans maturing and your hopes increasing, with your lover aiding and abetting. How long would you have waited before killing David?'

She said: 'I am going to shoot you.'

'There are a lot of things you're going to do,' said Rollison. 'Among them you're going to talk freely. Where does Pomeroy come in this, where does the Countess come in, where—'

'Look out!' cried Farrow.

He shouted as Gwendoline snatched the gun from the bag and, watching her closely, Rollison flung himself to one side. Renfrew, uttering a hoarse cry, rushed towards the door. Farrow shot out a leg and tripped him up—and Gwendoline fired.

A bullet passed between Farrow and the Toff, another was nearer the Toff as he went forward and the third hit the floor as he reached her and struck her arm down. He twisted her wrist until she gasped in pain and the gun dropped. But she was not finished yet. She pulled herself free and then flung herself bodily at him, gouging at his eyes, kicking at his shins and trying to knee him in the groin but he got a grip on her wrists at last and forced her away from him. She stood like that, bent forward, the breath hissing between her clenched teeth. Behind them Farrow was standing over a prostrate Renfrew.

There was a wild banging on the door and the receptionist screamed:

'Help! Help! Let me in, let me in! Help!'

'Keep her quiet,' said Rollison to Farrow and the "footman" went towards the door while Renfrew dragged himself painfully to his feet and Gwendoline dropped into a chair. He picked up her gun and motioned with it to Renfrew, making the man join Gwendoline. Renfrew stood beside her with one hand pressed heavily on the desk.

'And telephone Superintendent Grice,' Rollison called to Farrow.

Renfrew gasped: 'Rollison, you're wrong. We—we didn't do anything; Hilda has a weak heart, she might die at any time, I tell you she might die at any time!'

'With help from adrenaline,' said Rollison, coldly.

'That wasn't me, that was Farrow!'

'Not Farrow,' said Rollison. 'Renfrew, if Hilda dies you'll hang— *unless* you turn King's Evidence. You might escape death if you do that.'

'Don't talk to him,' muttered Gwendoline. Her eyes were bloodshot and she was still breathing through her mouth.

Rollison said: 'You had planned this before Pomeroy came along, hadn't you? And Pomeroy discovered what you were doing and saw a way of turning it to his advantage; Pomeroy was doing Barrington-Ley's accounts—' He broke off for a moment and then his voice grew stronger and there was a note of elation in it. 'I've got it! The simple things! The Relief Fund money was going through Barrington-Ley's accounts, like a dozen other charity funds, the American money was rightly transferred here, Pomeroy was after it, he could best get it by falsifying the main accounts, appropriating the money but making it look as if Barrington-Ley had used it. The rumours about his financial difficulties were spread to make that look convincing—and what a chance for you, sweet Gwendoline! How well Pomeroy would make it sound. You would kill Hilda, *he* would kill Barrington-Ley, because if the rich man lived the truth would one day out. For his risk Pomeroy had the Relief money, for yours you had the fine inheritance. Pomeroy didn't mention also that when you had it you would forever be in his power, did he?'

Gwendoline said, after a pause:

'It was all Pomeroy, all Pomeroy!'

'Yes!' cried Renfrew. 'Yes, we couldn't help ourselves!'

'You'd better rely on turning King's Evidence,' Rollison said. 'Denials won't help you and nothing will help Gwendoline. Let's have it Renfrew. You were in Pomeroy's confidence, weren't you— he could safely let you be in it and he wanted you to do so many things, such as killing the Countess. He was to murder Barrington-Ley and *you* were to swear that it was suicide. Come on, Renfrew! Take what chance you have!'

'If you—' began Gwendoline, grabbing Renfrew's arm. 'Yes!' screamed Renfrew. 'He made me do it, I couldn't help myself, it was Pomeroy, all Pomeroy.'

Then he began to talk, so swiftly and with such fluency that Rollison found it difficult to understand all he said. As he talked he damned Gwendoline so completely that she turned her bloodshot eyes away from Rollison and stared at the blank wall.

Farrow stood by the door, listening, saying nothing. He had pacified the receptionist and except for Renfrew's voice there was no sound in the room.

Renfrew had been desperately hard up and so had Gwendoline,

who received an allowance ample for her own needs but ridiculously small for his. His practice was small, for he had not been in Wimpole Street long, the expenses were enormous, his personal extravagance unlimited.

Barrington-Ley would not increase his daughter's allowance. Perhaps, thought Rollison, as he listened, David had some idea of the depths of evil that was in his daughter. She had evolved the plan to kill first Hilda and then her father; with Renfrew's help it should be easy, he could have signed the death certificates. Had the plot not spread wider, they might have succeeded and now be living in luxury. But into the black plot came Pomeroy, fat and genial and garrulous and above all dangerous. He came first because a company to whom Renfrew owed money had put the account into his hands. He appeared helpful and sympathetic and offered to advance money on expectations and Renfrew told him of Gwendoline and his hopes. Skilfully Pomeroy had drawn out of them the idea of murder, played on the theme and developed it; then whenever Renfrew showed signs of reluctance, used pressure because he knew the whole of Renfrew's financial plight.

In all of this, Gwendoline supported Pomeroy.

Pomeroy, keeping in the background at the Strand offices, visited Barrington-Ley, won his friendship, won the business for Pomeroy, Ward & Pomeroy, ingratiated himself and at the same time spread rumours here and rumours there.

There was some truth in the cry: '*It was all Pomeroy!*' Some, but not enough.

'It was Pomeroy,' said Renfrew, 'who had discovered that Lila, Countess Hollern, was in charge of the Relief Fund in New York, had influenced Barrington-Ley to sponsor the Fund in England, counting on willing assistance from Hilda. Pomeroy had arranged the transfer of the money and had the handling of it. Pomeroy put the whole foul plot into operation, conceived and executed it, with the help of Marcus Shayle and Malloy, of Janice Armitage although hers unwittingly. It was Pomeroy who, through Shayle, made Phyllis apply for a post at the Lawley Nursing Home—'

For the first time, Rollison interrupted.

'Could Pomeroy make sure that she got that post?'

'Of course he could!' cried Renfrew. 'The matron was in his power, she had been mixed up in one or two unsavoury cases. Pomeroy discovered it and made her do what he wanted. She said she would not go on after the attack on the Countess but she was persuaded to continue when the Countess recovered. Then Pomeroy sent Barrington-Ley there, the matron knew he was drugged, she was going to tell the police. Pomeroy killed her.'

Rollison said: 'She was poisoned with the same poison as that used on the Countess, at a time when Pomeroy, Shayle, and Malloy could not have got to the nursing home.'

'*I* didn't kill her!' gasped Renfrew. 'Rollison, you've got to believe me, I didn't kill her! I didn't give the Countess enough for a fatal dose, I couldn't really bring myself to kill Mrs Barrington-Ley!'

'But the matron was poisoned and she died,' said Rollison. He turned and looked at Gwendoline.

Renfrew cried: 'She knows where to get at my drugs.'

Gwendoline sprang at him as she had sprung at Rollison. Her fingers clawed his cheeks until the blood ran, she bit and kicked and scratched him until Rollison dragged her away. As she was struggling in his grip and Renfrew was leaning over the desk with his face buried in his hands, there were heavy footsteps outside and Grice led in his men.

CHAPTER TWENTY-ONE

My Lady's Memory

THERE WOULD BE bitter accusations and counter-accusations. Renfrew, Gwendoline, Pomeroy and Shayle would malign one another and try desperately to escape their rightful punishment. Gwendoline and perhaps Renfrew would be hanged, the others would get long terms of imprisonment.

Pomeroy had been afraid that Gwendoline would betray him and had instigated the attack on her—that had blinded them all to Gwendoline's activities. It was known, too, that when Lady Lost did not die, Shayle wanted Phyllis Armitage to find out whether she had really lost her memory. The firms of Pomeroy, Ward & Pomeroy were no longer practising and the principals and several members of the staff were under arrest.

The solvency of Barrington-Ley was now established beyond question and the run of selling on the Stock Exchange faded out. Barrington-Ley, who had been drugged by Pomeroy but not seriously, for it would not have suited Pomeroy had he died before his wife, was constantly by Hilda's bedside. Of her there were encouraging reports and on the fifth day she was past the crisis.

So Barrington-Ley told Rollison, when he called at the Gresham Terrace flat.

'I'm more than glad,' said Rollison.

'I know you are,' said Barrington-Ley. 'But for you—'

'I don't know that I covered myself with glory,' said Rollison. 'It's an old saw but a true one that the truth will out. Farrow, the man Hilda employed to find out what was happening, went a long way towards learning the truth.'

'There are a lot of things I don't know,' said Barrington-Ley, 'but I do know whom to thank. I wish there were a way of avoiding the trials, but—'

He stopped and Rollison knew that he was thinking of Gwendoline. However, there would always be Hilda for Barrington-Ley; his grief would be softened by her. The other man smiled, unexpectedly.

'I didn't come here to be melancholy! Rolly, somewhere in this business a letter from the Countess has been mentioned. I gather that it was supposed to have been written to me. I received business letters from her but I had never seen her until that night she arrived at the house. That is true, you know, whatever Renfrew said.'

'Of course it is,' said Rollison. 'No intrigue by David!'

'But it must have been written to someone,' said Barrington-Ley, reasonably.

'Yes,' said Rollison. 'I think she will know. She's better in everything but her memory and I shall give her the letter later this evening.' He was smiling but there was a look in Barrington-Ley's eyes which suggested he knew the smile was not a reflection of Rollison's real feelings.

The financier took his leave and then stopped at the door, by which Jolly was standing, to say that he had employed Phyllis Armitage to nurse Hilda and that when the nursing home was free from police surveillance, as it would be soon, Phyllis might become the new matron. Then he went off, this man who was always striving to do good, to his wife and with his memories, while Rollison went back into the living-room and Jolly asked:

'Is there anything more you require, sir?'

'What time did the Countess say she was coming back?' asked Rollison.

'At half-past six, sir. It is now a quarter-past.'

'Thanks.' Rollison looked out of the window, frowning, and then said: 'We don't know who sent me that photograph, Jolly. We do know that Renfrew sent the letter in my name and that one of Malloy's men was to have killed the Countess on her way here, an attempt which didn't come off, but the photograph remains a mystery.'

'I think it will be easily solved, sir,' said Jolly.

'By whom?'

'Well, sir, we have evidence that Mrs Barrington-Ley was seriously perturbed or she would not have resorted to a private detective agency. The photograph was not necessarily taken in London, since Renfrew lied about that to incriminate Mr Barrington-Ley further. There seems a possibility that a photograph might be sent from America so that the Countess could be identified—it would be a simple precaution, I'm sure you agree. As Mrs Barrington-Ley was the chief organiser for this particular Relief Fund in London, she was the most likely recipient of such a photograph.'

'Great Scott!' exclaimed Rollison.

'Exactly, sir,' murmured Jolly. 'The love-letter, if you remember, was shown to Mrs Barrington-Ley by Miss Gwendoline, so Mrs Barrington-Ley certainly suspected that the Countess was involved with Mr Barrington-Ley. What would be more natural than for Mrs Barrington-Ley to send you the photograph?'

Rollison said slowly: 'Nothing, Jolly. But why should Gwendoline turn up when she did?'

'Because she discovered what her mother had done and was anxious to find out whether you were interested, sir. She told you *her* story, confident that it would mislead you.'

'I think you're almost certainly right,' said Rollison.

A rather hysterical letter arrived that afternoon from Hilda: she had sent the photograph, she did hope Rollison forgave her; she had suspected David and dared not tell Rollison or *any*one the whole truth. There were other things mentioned and Rollison and Jolly sifted them from the irrelevancies which abounded in the letter. Hilda had employed Farrow and Pomeroy had discovered that without knowing what Hilda wanted Farrow to do. She had liked Pomeroy. He said that it was a splendid idea.

'And then saw in Farrow a fine Aunt Sally,' murmured Rollison. 'Well, that's clear now.'

'One thing *does* puzzle me, sir—the attack on Miss Gwendoline.'

'If the truth does come out,' said Rollison, 'I think we shall find that Pomeroy grew alarmed, because she was losing her grip, and he thought her better dead. If we don't learn the truth, we shall have to assume that.'

Rollison was looking out of the window and he stepped forward to see more clearly. Jolly stared at him.

The front door bell rang a few seconds afterwards.

'Thank you, Jolly!' said the Lady of Lost Memory, gaily. 'Is Mr Rollison in?'

'Yes, Madam,' said Jolly.

Rollison turned to greet her as she entered. She was wearing a simple dress of stone colour trimmed with maroon red, and a tiny hat of maroon red and shoes to match—for her luggage had been found at Malloy's house. It was known now that she had arrived in England a week before the *Bal Masque* and that Pomeroy had met her and taken her to Malloy.

Flo Malloy, knowing that her husband and the others planned to murder Lady Lost, had frustrated several attempts. Then she had realised there was no hope while the woman remained at the East End house. Flo had found the dress and the coat, the only garments Malloy had not locked away, and helped her to escape.

But for Flo, the Lady of Lost Memory would not have lived. When they had discovered her escape, Malloy and Pomeroy had gone *post haste* to Barrington House for Lady Lost had known of the *Bal Masque* that evening. One of them had followed her into the grounds, attacked her and been disturbed by a couple strolling through the shrubbery. She had been knocked out—and, on recovery, had remembered nothing. Attracted by the lights, she had gone into the house.

She knew little of what had been happening since then.

Now her eyes were shining and her cheeks were glowing. She held out her hands to Rollison, who took them and laughed with her, although there was pain in seeing her so happy.

'Memory back?' he demanded. They could joke about it now.

'I keep recalling little things,' she said. 'One day it will all come back. It *must* come back!' she repeated and sat down on the arm of a chair, her smile fading. 'I have been to see Mrs Barrington-Ley. She is so kind. She wishes me to stay with her, and'—there was a hint of laughter in her voice—'I cannot stay *here* much longer or all your friends will think badly of you!'

'Let them think,' said Rollison.

'I shall hate to go,' she said, 'but I must, and soon. You understand, don't you?'

'Of course,' said Rollison. 'I have been wrong to let you stay for so long.' He took the folded letter from his pocket, handed it to her and spoke carefully. 'Before you go, read that. It might bring something to your mind. It was found by the police. I read it because'—he paused—'because I had to.'

She took it, obviously puzzled. She unfolded it, saw the opening words and looked up at him, a new expression in her eyes. It was one

almost of fear—perhaps of fearful hope. She began to read but she
had not read more than half the letter before she crushed it in her
fingers and jumped up. On her face was a radiance which Rollison
had hoped to see but not because of this.

He made himself speak.

'You remember?'

'I remember! It is coming back, everything is coming back! My
husband is in Paris, this letter which I wrote to him was not received.
It must have been placed in an envelope sent to London. Where did
you find it?'

'It was at Barrington House.'

'But I did not write there,' she said, 'I wrote always to Mr
Barrington-Ley at the firm of Pomeroy, in the Strand. How did this
get to Barrington House?'

'Pomeroy probably took it there,' said Rollison.

'Of course! Poor Paul, how disappointed he was not to receive my
weekly letter!' She was in great spirits and moved about the room
excitedly.   'I remember everything! Paul—my home—New York
everything, everything; It is glorious! It is wonderful!' She stopped
suddenly, then moved towards him, took his hands in hers and kissed
Rollison. He held her very tightly and only when he felt her stiffen
did he release her, afraid that he had given himself away.

But she was suddenly filled with great alarm.

"Mr Rollison! I remember now, in New York I learned that this man
Pomeroy intended to do harm to Mr Barrington-Ley. A man whom he
knew asked for my aid in deception, I refused it; immediately I sailed
for London. There was a horrid week in a small house, where I saw
Pomeroy. We must warn—'

'There's no need to warn anyone,' said Rollison. 'It's all over.'

'Are you sure?'

'I'm quite sure,' said Rollison.

'I'm so glad,' the Lady of Lost Memory said. Then, after a pause:
'Poor Paul! He will be frantic because he has not heard from me for
so long. I must telephone him.' She looked towards the telephone
and Rollison, turning so that she could not see his eyes, went to it,
lifted the receiver, dialled and said:

'I want a Continental number, please.'

Have you read *The Toff and the Curate?*

Ronald Kemp was the new curate in a rough part of town. His face didn't fit and, when one of his parishioners was accused of murder, he didn't hesitate to call for help from The Toff. But Rollison had his work cut out trying to solve the mystery surrounding St Guy's—and preventing his hot-headed charge from making matters worse.

'I don't fight *h*infants,' declared Billy, scowling. 'But I wouldn't mind knocking the grin orf yer face, parson. Talk, that's all you're good for. Standin' up in the poolpit an' shouting yer marf orf—that's all yer can do. "Please Gawd, make me an' all me flock good lickle boys an' gels," ' continued Billy, in a fair imitation of the worst type of clerical drawl. 'Please Gawd—'

Kemp said quietly:

'Don't say that again.'

Billy broke off, looking at the curate in surpise. Kemp had gone pale and his fists were clenched.

It was the little man who broke the silence again, piping:

'Strewth! Have yer gorn sorft, Billy? *'It* 'im!'

'I don't like knocking *h*infants about,' repeated Billy. Something in Kemp's expression had stopped him and he was obviously on edge. It was Rollison's cue and he moved forward.

'You do a bit of boxing, Billy, don't you?'

'A bit!' squeaked the little man. 'Why there ain't a man in London can stand a round against 'im!'

'I can use me mits,' declared Billy the Bull, on safer ground. 'But this apology fer a parson only shoots 'is mouth orf, that's all. Cissy-boy!' he added. 'You ought to be back 'ome, wiv' yer muvver!'

'I'll fight you anywhere you like, under the Queensberry Rules,' Kemp said, tense-voiced.

'Coo, 'ear that?' squeaked the little man, dancing up and down. ''Ee's 'eard o' Lord Queensb'ry. Coo! Ain't 'e a proper little man! Why yer don't know wot fightin' is!'

'Don't be rash,' Rollison advised Kemp, 'Billy's an old campaigner.'

'I'll fight him anywhere he likes,' Kemp said again."

The Toff and the Curate, published July 2004. For more details of this and John Creasey's other books, visit www.johncreasey.com